PEEPING BEAUTY

PEEPING

written and illustrated by
MARY JANE AUCH

Holiday House/New York

Copyright © 1993 by Mary Jane Auch
ALL RIGHTS RESERVED
Printed in the United States of America

Library of Congress Cataloging-in-Publication Data
Auch, Mary Jane.
Peeping Beauty / Mary Jane Auch.
p.   cm.
Summary: Poulette the dancing hen falls
into the clutches of a hungry fox,
who exploits her desire to become
a great ballerina.
ISBN 0-8234-1001-3
[1. Chickens—Fiction.   2. Foxes—Fiction.   3. Ballet dancing—
Fiction.]   I. Title.
PZ7.A898Pe   1993   92-16374   CIP   AC
ISBN 0-8234-1170-2 (pbk.)

ISBN-13: 978-0-8234-1001-9 (hardcover)   ISBN-10: 0-8234-1001-3 (hardcover)
ISBN-13: 978-0-8234-1170-2 (paperback)   ISBN-10: 0-8234-1170-2 (paperback)

BEAUTY

Poulette wanted to be a famous ballerina. Every morning, while Gertrude and Philomena gossiped, Poulette did warm-up stretches and dreamed of stardom.

In the afternoon, while Claudine and Zelda scratched in the garden, Poulette danced her heart out.

"You're nuts," said Claudine. "Who ever heard of a dancing hen?"

"I'll be the first," said Poulette. "I have to follow my dream."

One day a fox appeared. "I've been watching you from my hill," he said to Poulette. "You have talent. Have you ever performed onstage?"

Poulette shook her head. "I've only danced around the farm. But I plan to be famous someday."

"I can help you!" the fox exclaimed. "I happen to be a talent scout in New York City. Right now, I'm hiring dancers for a new ballet called *Peeping Beauty*. Come audition for me tomorrow night."

"We hens never go off with strangers," said Poulette. "Especially strange foxes."

But a few days later, the fox was back. "I have everything ready," he said. "I've even built a special stage for you on my hill."

Poulette thought about her future. "I'd love to dance on a real stage," she said, "but you're a fox. How do I know you really want to help me?"

"Follow me," said the fox. "I have another surprise for you." He whipped something out from behind a rosebush. "I brought this tutu from New York especially for you. Isn't it stunning?"

"It's beautiful," Poulette said. "I'd love to dance in it . . . but I'll have to think about it."

The fox disappeared and came back a few hours later with a poster. "I've put these up all over town. Everyone wants to see you perform tonight. You can dance for a real audience."

"You'll be on a poster one minute and on a platter the next," clucked Claudine.

"Picture it," said the fox. "Hundreds of people will watch you dance. And when you take your bows, the audience will rise to its feet and applaud."

"Applaud for me?" asked Poulette. "Do you really think they will? Oh, I can't wait!"

"And after your performance, we'll have a lovely dinner," called the fox as he dashed up the hill. "Just the two of us."

"But only one of you will be eating," Zelda warned. "And it won't be you, Poulette."

"Stop trying to spoil my big chance!" snapped Poulette. "The fox wouldn't go to all this trouble just to eat me. You silly hens can spend your lives laying eggs and scratching for bugs, but I have talent. Tonight I'll become a star!"

When Poulette reached the stage that night, she was greeted by the fox.

"Why are you dressed like that?" she asked.

"You need a partner. I'll be the prince."

"Did lots of people come to see me dance?" Poulette peeked through the curtain, but she was blinded by the bright lights.

"There's not an empty seat out there. The whole audience is waiting for you to begin." The fox put on the music.

As the first notes floated over the stage, Poulette was no longer an ordinary hen. She became the lovely young princess, Peeping Beauty, and danced the best performance of her life.

"It's time for Peeping Beauty to fall asleep now," said the fox in a stage whisper. "Then I'll kiss you awake and we'll dance the finale."

Poulette pretended to prick her wing on the spindle. After a series of dizzying turns, she swooned onto a couch in center stage.

She waited for the fox's kiss, but nothing happened. When she opened her eyes, the fox's lips weren't puckered up at all. His sharp teeth glinted in the spotlight.

Poulette started to get up. "The finale!" she gasped.

"This *is* the finale," he said. "It's also the dinner, and you're the main course."

"You can't eat me in front of an entire audience," shrieked Poulette.
"There *is* no audience," said the fox.
"Then surely you couldn't eat a hen as talented as me."
"A chicken dinner is still a chicken dinner, no matter how talented she is,"
said the fox.

Suddenly Poulette had an idea. "All those hours of practice have made my muscles strong and hard . . . and tough. They don't call me 'thunder drumsticks' for nothing!" she shouted.

In one quick, graceful move, Poulette leaped up and did a *tour jeté*, knocking over the fox. "You're not having me for dinner, buddy. Your hen-eating days are over!"

The fox struggled to his feet, but Poulette was too fast for him. Before he knew what was happening, she toppled him with a *grand jeté*. He rolled over the edge of the hill. Poulette chased him all the way to the bottom.

The fox tumbled to a stop against the chicken coop. The other hens came running.

"All this exercise has made me hungry," said Poulette. "I think we should have fox for dinner."

"That's ridiculous," said the fox. "Chickens don't eat foxes."

"Who says?" asked Gertrude. "There's no law against it. Let's have fox chops with applesauce."

"Or maybe roast fox with chestnut stuffing," suggested Philomena.

"Let's have a picnic," said Zelda. "We'll grill foxburgers."

The fox tried to get up, but the hens jumped on top of him. "How can you say these things?" he cried. "I'm not a meal. I'm a fox . . . with feelings!"

"What am *I*, chopped chicken liver?" yelled Poulette. "You didn't think about *my* feelings when I was going to be *your* dinner."

"That's different," said the fox.

"I see," said Poulette. "Zelda, go get our roasting pan. Gertrude, you start the fire."

"No!" howled the fox. "Please let me go. I'll do anything."

"You promise you'll never eat another hen?" asked Poulette.

"No hens, I promise! No roosters, no ducks, no turkeys, no geese! I'll become a vegetarian!"

The hens laughed as they let the fox escape.

"Do you think he'll keep his word?" asked Gertrude.

"Probably not," said Poulette. "A fox is still a fox, no matter what he promises. But a talented hen will never be a chicken dinner."

RODIN

Rodin

by Yvon Taillandier

CROWN TRADE PAPERBACKS - NEW YORK

Title page: Eugène Carrière
PORTRAIT OF RODIN, 1898
Oil on canvas
Musée Rodin, Paris
(Gift of the sculptor Dervillez)

Series published under the direction of:
MADELEINE LEDIVELEC-GLOECKNER

Translated from the French by:
ANNE ROSS and A. CLARKE

Published by Crown Trade Paperbacks, 201 East 50th Street, New York, New York 10022.
Member of the Crown Publishing Group.

Random House, Inc. New York, Toronto, London, Sydney, Auckland

CROWN TRADE PAPERBACKS and colophon are trademarks of Crown Publishers, Inc.
Originally published in hardcover by Crown Publishers, Inc., in 1977.

Printed in Italy - Poligrafiche Bolis S.P.A., Bergamo

Library of Congress Cataloging-in-Publication Data
Taillandier, Yvon.
Rodin.
(Crown art library)
Bibliography
1. Rodin, Auguste, 1840–1917—Criticism and
interpretation. 2. Sculpture, French. 3. Sculpture,
Modern—19th century—France. 4. Sculpture, Modern—
20th century—France. I. Title. II. Series.
NB553.R7T3 1987   730'.92'4   87-23351

ISBN 0-517-88378-3

10 9 8 7 6 5 4 3 2 1

First Paperback Edition

LANDSCAPE IN THE FORÊT DE SOIGNES, n.d. Carboard 10⅝″ × 14″ (27 × 35.5 cm). Musée Rodin, Paris

UPROAR IN THE ROTUNDA

The woman was naked and her fingers were groping in the vain hope of covering her back. A man approached and glanced at her protruding bones, her flat chest, her lowered, ravaged face and her body seated on an unidentifiable lump which looked like mud. Was it really mud? He gave up the idea of finding out and turned away with an expression of disgust. In another part of this infernal place, two enormous legs supported the trunk of a colossus. The giant was swooping down upon the crowd. "Master," began a little girl in a worried voice, when a shout of "Butcher!" interrupted her. "Master," she continued, without apparently having noticed the interruption —

THE WALKING MAN, 1877. Bronze, h. 33½″ (85 cm)
The Metropolitan Museum of Art, New York. Gift of Miss G. Louise Robinson

"Master." But the wave of mutterings and unpleasant remarks once more drowned her treble voice. Her mentor, a stocky man of sixty whose admirers compared his beard to that of Michelangelo's Moses, and whom some unknown voice had accused of being a butcher, bent down toward the child. "Master," she repeated once more, this time making herself heard and pointing to the metal giant plunging down on the crowd without crushing anyone because, like Zeno's arrow which flew without flying, he was walking without walking, "Why hasn't he got a head?" It was the year 1900 in Paris, and the World Fair was at its height. On the corner of the Alma Bridge, in a rotunda, or round hall, where he had assembled more than two hundred works in marble, plaster, and bronze, François Auguste René Rodin, who is regarded today as the father of modern sculpture, was wandering with his young companion through the noisy throng of visitors and ordinary people who were just as lively, teeming and aggressive as the statues he had created. Without apparently attaching much importance to them, since he smiled continuously, he was observing the public's reactions. To judge by the exclamations, some of which he could hear, there was no doubt that in spite of his world-wide fame, his figure of an old woman weighed down with years and his headless giant standing 7 ft tall (with a head he would have measured more than 8 ft) were the cause of an uproar.

A MARTYR TO INCOMPLETION

This public outcry surprises us today. Why were these works considered scandalous, as if they were likely to set a bad example? They admittedly did set an example and were subsequently used as models; they stimulated a spirit of invention and led to the creation of revolutionary works by other sculptors. Thinking about the decrepit old woman, I am reminded of Germaine Richier's corroded sculptures, produced forty years after the uproarious scene in the rotunda. As for the headless giant, who without moving created such a strong and perplexing illusion of walking, I cannot help relating him to Giacometti's filiform walkers, first shown to the public forty years later, yet walking with the same joyful, determined step. He acquired fervent and distinguished admirers as soon as he appeared, or very soon after, notably a celebrated poet who was Rodin's secretary, Rainer-Maria Rilke, and a young man who was to become one of the most effective sculptors after Rodin, Brancusi. There are, however, not only admirers who talk, like Brancusi, or write, like Rilke. There are also those who prove their admiration by their works. Around that time, walking figures began to proliferate throughout the world of sculpture, and this trend, inspired by a walker lacking head and arms — for his decapitation is accompanied by this double mutilation — was not the work of insignificant people. Rather, it was Henri Matisse, the greatest of the Fauves, who,

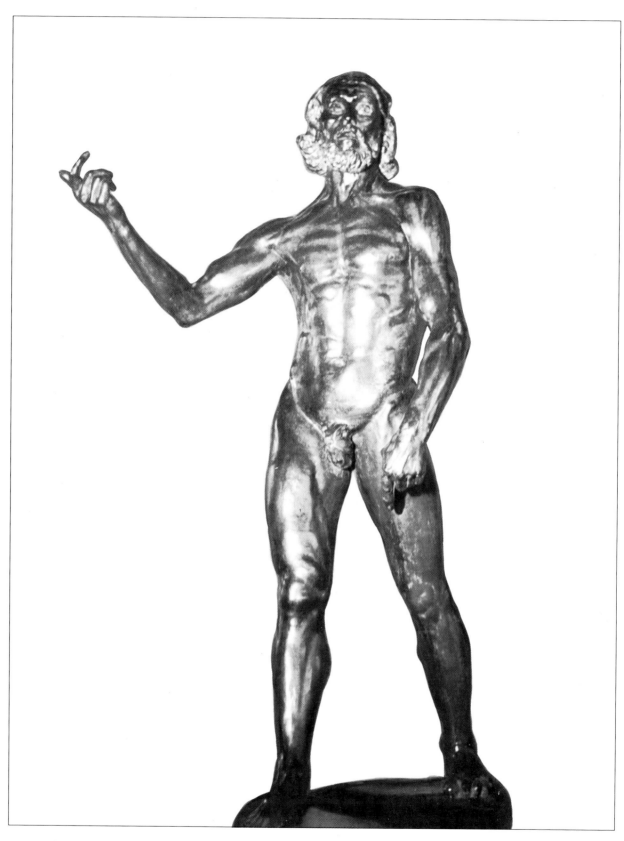

ST. JOHN THE BAPTIST PREACHING, 1877. Bronze, h. 79¹⁵⁄₁₆″ (203 cm). Musée Rodin, Paris

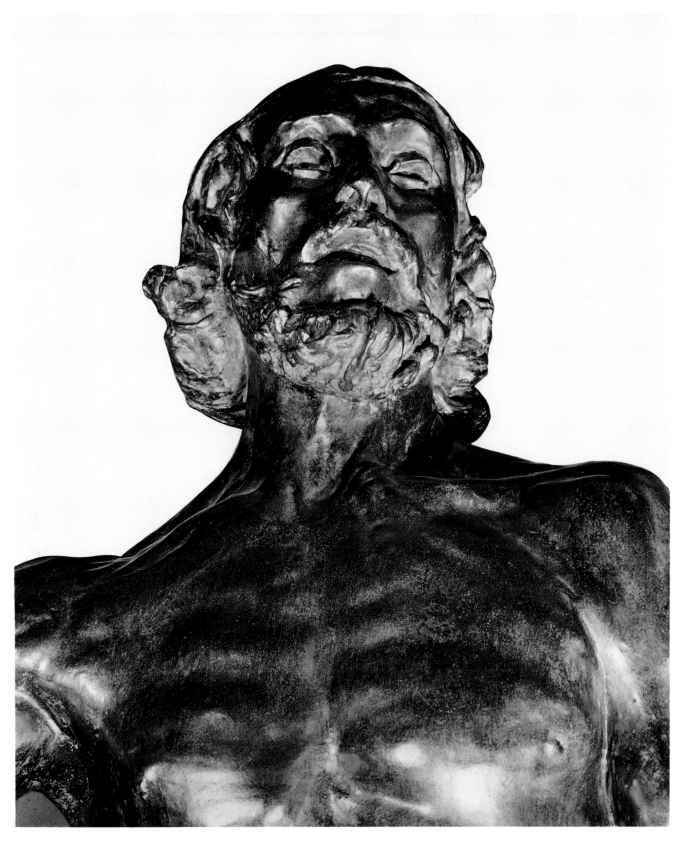

Detail from page 8

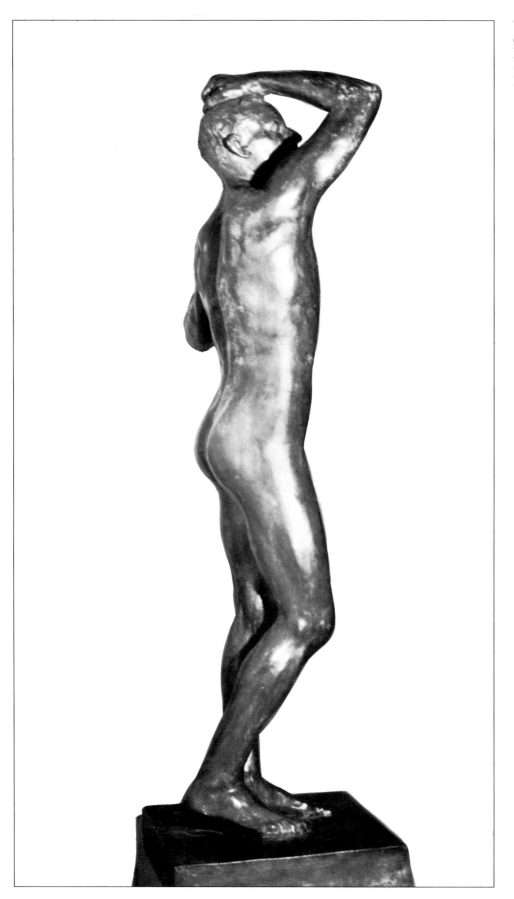

THE AGE
OF BRONZE, 1876
Bronze, h. 71½″
(181 cm)
Musée Rodin, Paris

in 1903, in his brief period as a sculptor, made a statue called *The Serf*. Brancusi said that in *The Walking Man (see page 6)* he admired the way in which a volume (the headless, armless trunk) has been placed in space, that is, projected by two legs set apart in a way calculated to form the outline either of an inverted capital Y, whether one looks at him in profile, full-face or from the back, or of a fork with its prongs buried in the earth. Matisse's *Serf*, while less mutilated than Rodin's walking figure (he has a head and upper arms, though his forearms are missing), also stands with his legs apart, forming the same upturned Y. There is also an odd character dated 1913 by Boccioni, one of the founders of the Futurist movement, who looks like a mass of wood shavings blown by the wind into the form of a person without arms, with a sort of head, walking in a way which produces the same inverted Y or the fork with downturned prongs. The same figure is to be found in *The Merry-Go-Round Pierrot*, also sculpted in 1913, by Archipenko, one of the first sculptors to use nothing but geometrical elements in his statues.

The little girl who in 1900 asked the sixty-year-old Rodin why his armless giant had no head had been too modest to notice that his sexual organs, at least in certain lights, seemed insignificant and partially effaced. If she had asked about this too, he would have replied that this did not make his giant any less potent. And indeed, he is still procreating, because I recently saw in the studio of one of the best sculptors of today, Jacques Delahaye, a walking figure with thighs only which otherwise closely resembled Rodin's man. Moreover, in a posthumous appraisal of Rodin as the father of modern sculpture, the headless, armless giant occupies an important position which is not attributable solely to his physical dimensions. Sixty-two years after the scene at the World Fair, the preface to a catalogue for an exhibition of seventy-two small sculptures and forty-two drawings by Rodin at the Minneapolis Art Institute summarizes the posthumous prestige of the great sculptor. "For twenty years, from 1930 at 1950," writes the anonymous author, "Rodin became unfashionable among artists, who in their purely formal experience found the drama and passion in his work embarrassing, but some years ago he was rediscovered." The writer adds that Rodin marks a pinnacle in the history of Western art. He was harshly criticized during his lifetime, as was Picasso during his lifetime only to receive recognition later. This catalogue contained only one illustration, but the single work chosen to represent the whole output of the greatest sculptor of the nineteenth century is neither *The Age of Bronze*, nor *St. John the Baptist Preaching*, nor the prodigious *Balzac*, nor one of *The Burghers of Calais*, impressive though they all are, but *The Walking Man* without a head.

A year later, Parisians saw two exhibitions devoted to Rodin's works, one at the Louvre and the other at a gallery specializing in sculpture, where the pieces shown had been strictly chosen so as to satisfy lovers of the avant-garde. A few years before her death in 1959, Germaine Richier told me that in her opinion the greatest sculptor of all was Rodin. "But," she added, "that may make me sound a little old-fashioned." The avant-gard gallery certainly did not wish to appear old-fashioned. Among the works selected was the headless giant. If nowadays we find this headlessness hardly surprising, we are at fault. This work could be called, as Rodin called his monument to Balzac, the very pivot of his concept of beauty. The omission of this, the highest part of man's anatomy, played a decisive role in the evolution of contemporary sculpture and it also imparted to the headless creature a remarkable symbolic plentifulness. This is why, amid the tumult of the puzzled, angry visitors to the rotunda, the little girl was quite right to ask respectfully, "Master, why hasn't he got a head?" In his work entitled "Discovery of Modern Sculpture", Jean Selz remarks that the mutilation of *The Walking Man* has given rise to the criticism that Rodin was incapable of finishing a work. This reproach would seem annoying today, because incompleteness is no longer necessarily considered a fault. Edgar Degas, a contemporary of Rodin and an Impressionist, said ironically of the many pictures whose "finish" excited admiration, "Certainly they have been finished, but can one really say that they were ever begun?" This quip became famous, and now it is felt that incompleteness in the aesthetic sphere is not a sign of insufficiency but rather a powerful means of arousing emotion or interest. For we are living in a world of beginnings; our impression is not that humanity is achieving great things, but rather initiating them. We live in a world of invention, and a meditative person likes his inventive faculties to be stimulated in his encounters with art.

This is precisely the effect of incompletion. When one contemplates the unfinished *Walking Man*, just because he has neither arms nor head one can imagine that this is not a Rodin, but some ancient statue decapitated and shorn of its arms by the ravages of time. Perhaps, the example of so many mutilated Greek and Roman statues which Rodin admired so much — such as the armless *Venus of Milo* and the headless *Victory of Samothrace* — seemed to him sufficient authorization for the mutilation of his bronze walker. As Rodin said, "Antiquity is supreme beauty." In the rotunda at the 1900 World Fair, observant visitors might have noticed a strange couple embracing (*see page 20 for the marble version*). Were they a man and a woman, or two women? They are in fact a man and a woman, but the man in undergoing a metamorphosis, changing into a woman. And what if the *Victory of Samothrace*, which seems to sail at the prow of a ship as *The Walking Man* seems to walk at the prow of some unidentified vessel, were herself to change sex? She might perhaps lose part of her wings and the damp garment which clings to her body, but would probably retain the stubs of her wings, which closely resemble the embryo arms on the torso of the bronze giant.

THE GATES OF HELL, 1880-1917.   Bronze, h. 20′ 9³⁄₁₆″ (635 cm).   Musée Rodin, Paris

Detail from page 15

However, incompletion does not only send one back in time; it also draws one into a conspiracy with the future. One does not only ask, "What were his arms like? What sort of face did he have? In what disaster or what struggle did he lose them?" One too wonders, thinking, "This creature has not any arms yet. Perhaps I should make them grow, but how, and what should they be like? As for his head, if I had to mould it, what features would I give him?" In short, one's mind, stimulated by incompletion, sees it as suggesting either destruction or construction, depending on whether one looks at it in terms of the past or the future, and one feels drawn to participate in the act

THE THINKER, 1880.   Bronze, h. 28¼″ (71.9 cm).   Musée Rodin, Paris

THE THREE SHADES, 1881.   Bronze, h. 38¼″ (97.2 cm).   Musée Rodin, Paris

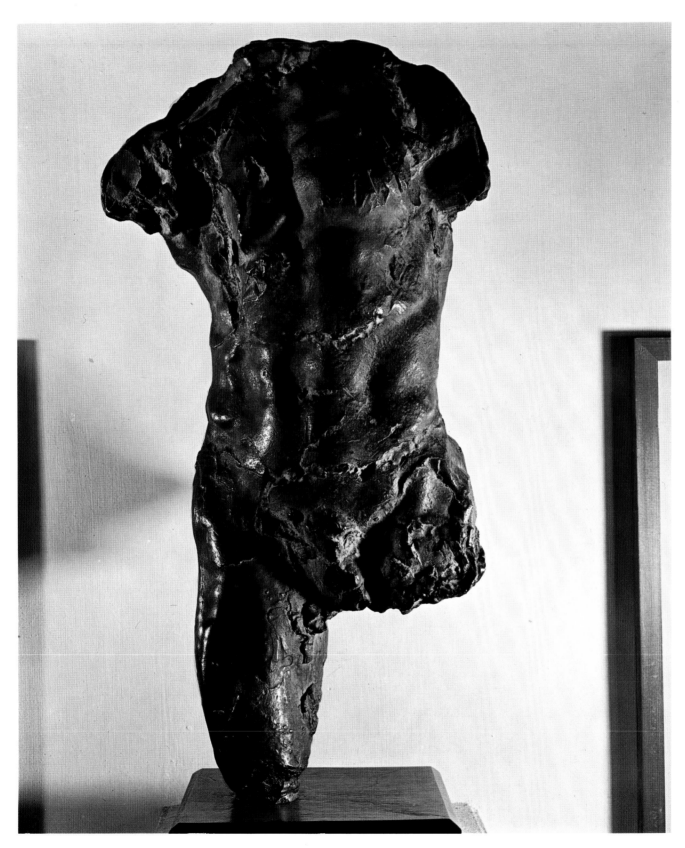

MALE TORSO, 1878.   Bronze, h. 20⅞″ (53 cm).   Petit-Palais, Paris

«I Am Beautiful» (The Abduction), 1882. Bronze, h. 27¾″ (70.5 cm). Rodin Museum, Philadelphia

MEDITATION, 1885. Bronze, h. 29⅛″ (74 cm). Musée Rodin, Paris

THE METHAMORPHOSES OF OVID, 1907-1912. Marble, h. 13¼″ (33.8 cm)
Ny Carlsberg Glyptotek, Copenhagen

of creation. This is very fashionable today. "Modular" works are being created, works which one can change by altering the position of certain movable parts, so that one tastes an element of creative excitement. Rodin himself wanted everyone in the world to be an artist, or at least to have access to the artistic world, if only through craftsmanship, the extinction of which he was already deploring. Such considerations were, of course, unknown to his detractors, who leveled at him the same reproach as that which they were leveling at Cézanne. In the same way their parents and grandparents had tried to crush Corot, who, in reply to those who wanted to know why his works were not finished, said (this riposte is also attributed to Vernet de Lyon), "And what do you do with infinity?"

a mon ami Bourdelle
Rodin

DANAID, HER HAIR

So the headless giant gives Rodin a place occupied by no previous sculptor except Michelangelo — that of a martyr to voluntary incompletion and, more widely, to that which is taken for formlessness. But since research into formlessness is a way to find form on a different level, this incompletion, or formlessness, of Rodin's was to give birth to countless new forms, and particularly to abstract, non-representational or obliquely representational form. In any case, the critics of this headless man, who is a true advocate of fertile incompletion, did not foresee that by carrying to its logical conclusion the principle behind the omission of the head and the arms and eliminating first the legs, then the division between chest and stomach, and finally the various distinguishing points which lead one to identify a human body, one would arrive at Brancusi's ovoid, at Arp's "smooth clouds" and at Stalhy's pillars of hypertrophied glands. If they had foreseen this, their horror would have made them doubly aggressive.

DANAID, 1889-1890. Marble, h. 14⅛″ (36 cm). Musée Rodin, Paris

STANDING WOMAN WITH HAND IN HAIR, n.d.
Graphite, estompe and watercolor, 12⅞″ × 9⅞″ (32 × 24.8 cm).   Musée Rodin, Paris

24

If one is not a masochist, to be the victim of aggression can hardly be a cause for satisfaction. Rodin's feelings may perhaps explain his clear, though unemphatic reaction. The little girl who questioned him in the rotunda still remembers very well, more than sixty years later, the tense and uncomfortable pressure of his fingers. In fact, of what was he accused? The incompletion — taken as unintentional — of his *Walking Man* and the ugliness of his old woman?

OBSESSION WITH TIME

"Master," the little girl had said, "why hasn't your giant got a head?" Rodin might have replied, "Perhaps because time has removed it." And if she had asked, "Why is your old woman so ugly?", he might have replied, "Because she was also a giant — a giant of beauty, whom François Villon celebrated in his poems. She was called 'La Belle Heaulmière', but time has passed and it has damaged her nearly as much as if it had beheaded her. It has left her in the state you see her in." Rodin took pleasure in describing Time as a butcher, even as he was accused of being one too. This is one of the reasons why some strange things happened in that rotunda, so that his little companion might have asked many other questions than the one about the headless giant. For instance, she might have asked, "What's that naked man doing on all fours?" Rodin would have replied, "That's a man eating his children. He is an ogre, a character from Dante's 'Inferno' called Ugolino, and the group consisting of him and his victims is an enlargement of a detail from *The Gates of Hell*." One can regard this ogre as a revival of the myth of Chronos or Saturn, the personification of Time, who also ate his own children. In any case Rodin might also have replied, "That's a self-portrait," because he seemed to devour or destroy his own works, like a modern Ugolino or Chronos. If the little girl, instead of looking straight up at the top of the giant, had, like a mountaineer who starts climbing from the bottom to reach the summit, looked first at his right foot, she might have seen a protruding piece of iron, which had been used to strengthen the structure when it was nothing but a mass of clay. This apparent carelessness was a stylistic effect which has since been revived, notably by Robert Couturier, in certain works that are almost reduced to a framework. In his giant, however, Rodin just hinted at the possibility of a similar treatment, and probably the little girl, who could not know what the consequences were to be half a century later, would have dismissed it as unimportant. She would have noticed that the rest of his feet and his calves, knees and thighs were shaped with the greatest care. Their surface is smooth and pleasant to the touch like a healthy skin. The swellings and indentations which mark the muscles and bones make a system of hills and valleys without sudden landslides or crevasses. From the top of his thighs, it all changes. Rodin, who respected anatomy ("Let anyone come and tell me if I have made an anatomical mistake") and admired the human body, loving its harmonies and carefully observing its smallest variations, metamorphosed himself into Chronos-Ugolino, giving the frightening impression of having grown fangs or talons. As though driven by a strange hunger, he looked on his own child, his creation, as something to destroy. The genitals are crushed, and on the stomach and the diaphragm the body is scored by two long, deep gashes which look like fractures. The back does not follow the usual contours of human physiology: the cleft dividing the buttocks is filled, while the buttocks themselves are by contrast caved in as though by a blow. On the flanks are strange pieces, perhaps bits of torn flesh, which, as they hang, seem to reweld themselves into the body. From the front one sees a kind of crater, partly filled in, at the level of the groin, bruises at the top of the left thigh, holes in the upper dorsal region and a large cavity shaped like a comma at the top of the right lung. At the base of the left lung there is a twisted place as though the flesh has been pinched and the mark has remained. There is also a great vertical cleft starting at the base of the chest and going up, like a sword or a dagger wound, from the vertebral area. Under the shoulder, seen from the side, there is a kind of fork which traces three deep lines, and, finally, both arms have been torn out like plants pulled out of the ground, so that appalling, palpitating whorls of flesh remain. Also, where the head has been removed there is a gaping wound which extends far beyond the surface of the neck to spread over the top of the torso in a great area of apparently putrid flesh. To make matters worse, these wounds seem to have been inflicted on a living person, and not on an unfeeling dead body as in an anatomy lesson. This is more than a sculpture, this is a human being, alive and upright, and the effect is that of the work of a torturer. "Butcher," someone in the rotunda had said.

It is said that Damian, in a moment of unbelievable masochism, at the end of long and terrible tortures, cried out, "More, more!" *The Walking Man*, no longer having a head, has no mouth with which to utter this fearful cry, but the very manner in which he stands so terribly upright, like a cockerel which still runs after being beheaded, seems to cry out, on behalf of his lost lips. (And this is not impossible. The Spanish painter Antonio Saura once told me a story of his childhood in Madrid during the Spanish Civil War. He was looking out of the window at an approaching pedestrian when all of a sudden, with a whistle, a bursting shell removed the passer-by's head. During that seemingly interminable moment, which must have lasted but a few seconds, he watched, his eyes dilated with horror, while the beheaded man continued to walk, like Rodin's giant). However, Jacques Bornibus wrote in the introduction to the Rodin exhibition at the Claude Bernard Gallery in Paris in 1963 that "any purely dramatic interpretation (of the tortured, headless giant) is irrelevant." So there is no drama in *The Walking Man*. This seems an unacceptable paradox, yet it is true. A sculpture should often stand at a distance from the spectator, as is also the case with the Impressionist paintings contemporary with Rodin. *The Walking Man* is dated 1877, and the first Impressionist exhibition at Nadar's took place in 1874, just three years before.

I remember one day seeing two women looking at a Pissarro painting. One was saying to the other, "From close up you see nothing, but from a distance it all falls into place." It is the same with Rodin, and more especially with *The Walking Man*. From a distance, it all falls into place, and Jacques Bornibus was perfectly right: "Any purely dramatic interpretation is irrelevant, because of the self-assurance of his posture and the obvious health of the body, which gives it vitality." From a few paces away this tortured body appears perfectly healthy.

Inside the Hôtel Biron, where part of the Rodin Museum collection is to be found (the rest is in the surroundings gardens and in a deconsecrated chapel at one end of the gardens), two walking figures face each other, moving motionlessly toward each other: *The Walking Man* and *St. John the Baptist (see page 8)*. One can imagine that these are the same person at two different moments in his life, since St. John the Baptist was to have his head cut off and presented to Herod on a platter. The same face represents two phases of this life — the radiant look of the Messenger of Christ and the downbeaten, corpse-like air of the condamned and beheaded man. However, to appreciate this one must undertake what I call in my book "Le Voyage de l'œil" an educational promenade, that is, come close, step back and come closer again, but never stand still. From a few paces away what one sees is the relation of high and low, as St. John the Baptist seems to gesture toward the walking man, commenting, "Look, his head has gone" and "Look, how alive his body still is." He thus seems to speak not only of the walking man but also of his own fate: "I began as a prophet; I shall be executed." This is also the dialogue or contrast between heaven and earth, between spirit and flesh. We shall see how Rodin resolved this conflict in the years from 1898 to 1900.

For the moment let us walk about to gather knowledge. From afar *(see page 8)* St. John the Baptist's head seems radiant, vital and forceful. From nearby *(see page 9)* it seems that life has already left it and that its movements are no longer human. All Rodin's bronze portraits are similar, like the face of *St. John the Baptist* and the body of *The Walking Man*, they portray torture if one examines them from close by and concentrates a little. They are all deepened, multiplied lines and accentuated features, recalling certain Byzantine portraits which look as though the skin has been stripped off them. To achieve the interplay of shafts of light on the facets, the flesh seems

FLEETING LOVE (FUGIT AMOR), 1886.   Marble, h. 24⅜″ (62 cm).   Musée Rodin, Paris

bruised, furrowed and torn.   In short, here is sadism once again.   I remember that
my youthful reaction to these portraits was to relish the tortures.   For a long time I
felt guilty about my feelings of pleasure, until the moment when I realized that there
is an irrepressible force in us which drives us to destruction.   One can conquer this
while seeming to submit to it, precisely through this type of delight which I felt in
front of Rodin's mutilated works, because it is better that a malevolent impulse should
be satiated in this way and exhaust itself in imagination, rather than demand of us
real torture and blood.   "This pleasure," I told myself, "is my way of attaining sincere
pacifism."   It may seem naive to presume that if the public had understood Rodin better

THE GOOD NEWS, n.d. Marble, h. 28¾″ (73 cm)
The Thyssen-Bornemisza Collection, Lugano-Castagnola, Switzerland

WOMAN WITH SWIRLING VEILS, c. 1890
Graphite, pen, red and brown ink and watercolor gouache, 6⅞″ × 4⅜″ (17.5 × 11 cm)
Musée Rodin, Paris

before the First World War and had loved his sadism instead of rejecting it hypocritically, there would have been no war, but one cannot help thinking that the same men who shouted "How horrible!" in front of *She Who Was the Helmet-Maker's Once Beautiful Wife (see page 76)*, who cried "Butcher!" at Rodin when they saw his *Walking Man*, and who thought the Impressionists, Cézanne, Van Gogh, Gauguin, Seurat, the Fauves and the Cubists hideous and frightful, soon after acquiesced in four years of world war, and that this divorce of art from the public coincided exactly with the escalation of armed conflict.

Rodin's beneficent sadism is not always as obvious as it is in his bronzes, such as the bust of *Alexandre Falguière (see page 36)* or *Alphonse Legros (see page 51)* or the portrait of *Clémentel* which I admired as a young man in the courtyart of the town hall at Riom. He does not always show himself so clearly as the reincarnation of the cruel Chronos — Time with his destroying scythe become sculptor. He sometimes speaks of Time more contemplatively or more sentimentally. The little girl so intrigued by the headless giant would also have been surprised by the acrobatics of a strange marble couple called *Fugit Amor (see page 28)*. The theme of the couple occurs frequently in Rodin's work, allowing him not only to express his sensuality but also from the technical point of view to create massive sculptures, only slightly perforated, which would have satisfied Michelangelo's maxim: "A statue thrown from the top of a mountain should arrive at the bottom unbroken." This massiveness also allowed Rodin (would Michelangelo have approved?) to stress the contrast between a very compact block and the arm or head which emerges from it. The couple bearing the title which evokes the transient nature of love lie on an almost unworked block of stone reminiscent of a bed, a rock worn by the tide or the tide itself, on which the man, lying on his back, is striving to hold on to a woman who is slipping away from him like a fish. She is not a siren, but an anti-siren, who is no longer trying to seduce him but to escape the bonds woven by her seduction. Time, which destroys love as it destroys life, has done its work.

However, Time to Rodin does not always have this destructive connotation. He also saw it in a recitative, historical sense and is thus a forerunner of what is today called narrative art. Talking with one of his intimates, he explained at length that painting and sculpture could in the context of history vie with literature and music, saying that sculpture belonged to the dimension of time as well as to that of space. He takes as an example of this the six *Burghers of Calais*, commissioned in 1885 and erected in 1895 *(see pages 46 and 47)*. The expression on the faces and in the attitudes of these six men who, in order to save their city, agreed to be executed by the victorious English can be considered in the narrative sense. In his movements and in facial expression each burgher personifies one of the various stages of a deliberation which began in despair

THE KISS, 1888-1898.   Marble, h. 72 1/16″ (183.6 cm).   Musée Rodin, Paris

and ended in stoical resolution. Each statue is thus the equivalent of a chapter in a book or a paragraph in a lecture. *The Walking Man* can also be regarded in this way, for not only is it legitimate to ask where he has come from, where he is going or even where he is (since a naked man walking without head or arms could hardly be found in a normal place) but also, to the little girl's question about his absence of a head, Rodin could have answered, "Because he is telling a story of destruction which unfolds like a three-act tragedy: Act One, The Legs — all is calm and smooth. Act Two, The Trunk — the body is attacked, hacked, torn (the action speeds up). Act Three, Mutilation and Execution — the head and arms disappear. In dramatic terminology this is called the Catastrophe." There was nothing to prevent Rodin from adding, "You will see. I have made another sculpture of the same type, a monument commissioned by the Committee of the Société des Gens de Lettres on July 6, 1891, at the suggestion of Emile Zola, who was then President of that body. It took me eight years to finish it. I exhibited it at the Salon de la Société nationale, and the Committee of the Société des Gens de Lettres refused it in the following terms: 'The Société des Gens de Lettres must regretfully protest against the rough draft which Monsieur Rodin is exhibiting at the Salon, since it refuses to recognize a statue of *Balzac* therein'."

"THE GARDEN OF TORTURES"

Balzac drank coffee, slept little, worked much. When he died at the age of fifty-one, he had an enormous stomach, and that is the central theme of the first draft of Rodin's monument to him. This protuberant abdomen gave the sculptor the opportunity to create one of those magnificent swelling volumes which, according to one of the greatest Cubist sculptors, Henri Laurens, looked like a juicy fruit. The rest of the figure, with its hypertrophied muscles, expresses strength and is a "tour de force", because Rodin has succeeded in making a resplendent figure out of a fifty-year-old who had never been handsome. At this point the monument could have been considered finished and the sculptor should have been satisfied. But obviously he was not, for he continued working. He wanted to dress *Balzac*. First he thought of putting him in a frock coat, but rejected the idea, and was not sure what to do. The voice of one of his assistants, and therefore the voice of a subordinate (like the serpent in Genesis and, like it, destined to become famous), suggested, "Master, why not drapery?" Rodin was too much a realist to dress a nineteenth-century writer in Greek or Roman robes, so the voice spoke again, "Why not a dressing-gown?" asked Bourdelle. The die was cast, and Rodin draped Balzac in his dressing-gown, though others called it a homespun sackcloth. Whatever the cloth, this vague mass, suggesting a natural rock, is hiding everything, arms, legs, stomach

THE PRODIGAL SON, before 1889.   Bronze, h. 54⅜″ (138.2 cm).   Musée Rodin, Paris

34

THE ETERNAL IDOL, 1888. Plaster, h. 28¹³⁄₁₆″ (73.2 cm). Musée Rodin, Paris

BUST OF ALEXANDRE FALGUIÈRE, 1897. Bronze, h. 17⅝″ (44 cm). Petit-Palais, Paris

(see page 89), leaving only the head free. This head, which is set on a strange geological phenomenon — a mountain, Miró called it — is another example of Rodin's "sadism." This is the same theme as in *The Walking Man*, but in reverse. If the little girl, instead of looking at the headless giant, had been looking at the disembodied novelist, she would certainly have asked, "Master, why hasn't he got a body?" and Rodin, ignoring the scholar's maxim that repetition is no explanation, could have answered, in order to dispose of a bothersome question, that *Balzac* and *The Walking Man* were not his only examples of execution and mutilation, or of showing wounds.

One of his first sculptures — one cannot help seeing an omen in this — is dated 1864, and is of a man with a broken nose. In 1885 he sculpted another man's head, not with a broken nose, but with the right ear missing. *The Walking Man* can be thankful to have two legs, because there is another bronze character whom one can see today in the Petit-Palais Museum in Paris *(see page 17)* and who looks like his brother in misfortune, since like his more famous relation he is missing his head and arms, and his chest and stomach bear the same wounds and ugly scars. If there is any joy in walking in this condition, he cannot know of it, for his left leg is totally missing and of his right all that remains is the thigh, on which he stands like a flower on its stalk. Even he should not complain, for if there is consolation to be found in the existence of a greater misfortune than one's own, it is his. There is a headless young girl who bears the marks of her hands on her flanks but is missing both arms and both legs. A headless young man of the same year — 1882 — is reduced to the same condition.

Any observer of Rodin's work who is at all attentive can note mutilated creatures in the stances of acrobats, like the headless woman who holds her right thigh in her right hand and has only a left forearm, stuck to her body, while her legs seem to be swimming or flying, since it is called *Flying Figure* (1891). Among many others, there are series of mutilated creatures. At the top of *The Gates of Hell (see page 13)* there are three figures, three men with bent heads, known as *The Three Shades (see page 16)*. They look exactly like each other, like triplets, but on close examination it can be seen that this similarity goes beyond that of triplets and that they are in fact one and the same person, seen from different angles, and that the group, sculpted in 1880, is really the analysis of one movement in its various stages, such as the Futurists were to portray thirty years later. Until now no sadism can be discerned in Rodin, but a closer look reveals that when sculpting this group of three figures, or three views of one figure in a more or less rectangular form, he made each of them bend his head beyond the limit of physical possibility, so that one is led to think of three hanged men who have been resuscitated but who show their recent suffering in the abnormality of their necks.

NUDE WOMAN SEATED, RIGHT PROFILE, n.d.
Pencil and watercolor wash, 11¾″ × 7⁷⁄₁₆″ (30 × 19 cm).   Petit-Palais, Paris

RED-HAIRED WOMAN STANDING, n.d.   Pencil and watercolor wash, 11¹³⁄₁₆″ × 7⁷⁄₁₆″ (30 × 19 cm)
Petit-Palais, Paris

PYGMALION AND GALATEA, 1889.   Marble, h. 38¼″ (97 cm)
The Metropolitan Museum of Art, New York. Gift of Thomas F. Ryan in memory of William M. Laffan

NIOBE, c. 1900.   Marble, h. 19½″ (49.5 cm)
The Toledo Museum of Art, Ohio

Even from a distance they are impressive, not only on account of this anomaly but particularly because their three left arms converge, as do three arms belonging to the fishermen-apostles in Raphael's *Miraculous Draft of Fishes*, as they draw the bursting net out of the water. Here the convergence of the arms was designed to draw attention to a small space on the canvas which otherwise would not have been noticed, at least at first glance, and which in fact was the tip of the miraculously filled net emerging from the water. In Rodin's composition the convergence fulfilled the same purpose. The three arms of *The Shades* form an arrow which directs attention toward *The Thinker* and the *Hell* on which he looks down. To make this arrow sharper still, Rodin, faithfully living up to the name of butcher given to him in the rotunda in 1900, has cut off their three left hands. But this is not all, for the arrow itself needs to be stressed, as it indeed is: this time not by three arms but by a leg belonging to one of *The Three Shades*, the knee of which is bent in such a way that it points to the three arms, which point to *The Thinker*, who in turn points toward *Hell*. So that the point of this knee should look like an arrow and its directional significance be clear, Rodin put his figures in a difficult, contorted position that emphasizes the limb which bears the weight and points in the desired direction. However, the right hand could have veiled the movement of the thigh. This method can be observed in another sculpture called *Adam* or *The First Man (see page 62)*, a reincarnation of *The Shades* but different, in that *The First Man* is not pointing at anything, his left arm falls vertically instead of being stretched out obliquely, and he has a right hand. Rodin ruthlessly cut off the Shade's right hand, and as *The Shades* are acknowledged to be a single person, so the amputation of one hand at the wrist has led to the amputation of two others. Thus *The Thinker* is in no danger of passing unnoticed, nor *Hell* of being forgotten.

THE DESTRUCTION OF CLASSICAL MAN

Who is *The Thinker* and what is this hell over most of which he broods, while a lesser part surrounds him without his seeming to be wholly its captive? The usual reply is that this is the hell of Dante's "Divine Comedy", but *The Thinker* is clearly contemplating the infernal regions. Is it likely that he knows Dante? I was wondering along these lines one day in the gardens of the Rodin Museum. To my left, in the open air, was *The Gates of Hell* with *The Thinker* in his small-scale form. To my right, on a raised pedestal, the same *Thinker*, but larger than life. Looking at these two intellectuals, the large and the small, the thought occurred to me that Dante was a classic, and that, to be acquainted with a classic, one has to have attended a class. Regardless of his size, *The Thinker* seemed to me in spite of his name a wholly physical being, to whom the so-called cultural sphere must have been completely foreign *(see pages 14 and 15)*.

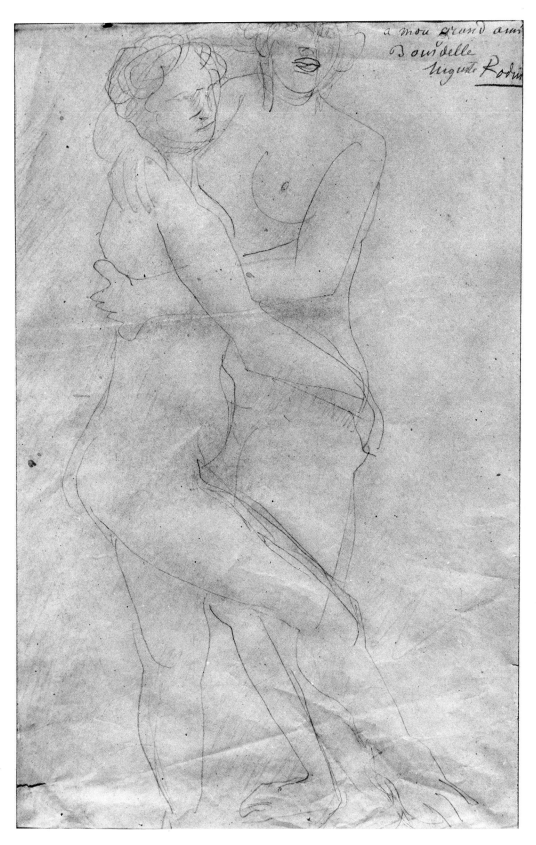

Two Women. Study, n.d.   Pencil and watercolor, 12″ × 7½″ (30.5 × 19 cm)
Musée Bourdelle, Paris

43

DESPAIR, 1890.   Bronze, h. 13⅜″ (34 cm).   Musée Rodin, Paris

NUDE SEEN FROM BEHIND, n.d.   Pencil, 12″ × 7⅞″ (30.6 × 20 cm).   Musée Rodin, Paris

THE BURGHERS OF CALAIS, 1884-1886. Plaster, h. 91⅛″ (231.5 cm). Musée Rodin, Meudon, France

In 1876, four years before he sculpted that powerful body in which intellectual culture and meditation seem so misplaced, Rodin modeled the upright body of a young man who had apparently just woken up. With the help of its title, *The Age of Bronze (see page 10)*, it is usually interpreted as a symbol of man's awakening to consciousness, but though youth goes well with the idea of awakening, it goes less well with that of human brutishness touched for the first time with subtlety of spirit. The brutishness, which is missing from *The Age of Bronze*, abounds in *The Thinker*. From some angles his outline is a zigzag line which recalls lightning and tempest, as though this seated man

THE BURGHERS OF CALAIS, 1884-1886.   Bronze, h. 90¹⁵⁄₁₆″ (231 cm).   Musée Rodin, Paris

was prey to some internal storm, or the personification of the storm itself in which the first human ideas were to be born. In other words, he would be a representative of prehistoric man, the caveman. Caves occur as a frequent theme in Rodin's work, in the principle of composition governing the "bracket" form he likes to use — a concave form which gives a cavernous or corolla-like scoop to the human body, making Rodin a forerunner of Pevsner. Rodin's works often suggest prehistoric art. His drawings, though they herald Matisse, look as though they have been scratched on the uneven surface of rock-caves. The separation of line and color, which reminds one of Dufy, powerfully evokes the dissociation produced in an image by movement, and movement is one of the characteristics of cave-drawings which most surprise the experts.

Is not *The Thinker* nude because he belongs to a society which had not yet invented clothes? But why did Rodin, in an age when clothing had long existed, persist in concentrating on that primitive era when man went about without any protective covering? Perhaps because he is a creator, and feels the vulnerability of his original ideas. Another sculpture, which at least in subject is the feminine counterpart of *The Thinker*, since she is entitled *Thought (see page 54)*, represents a female head just emerging from a rectangular prism of rough-hewn marble. This one could describe as thought struggling with matter — the allegory of the first stirrings of creative ideas. Creations has many other, equally challenging, stages, so why was Rodin especially interested in this one? All his incomplete marble statues can express the same idea — that of beginning or birth. To this question he replied that "a whole new world is pulsing". What is this world, still in prehistory? What is its connection with *The Thinker* and *The Gates of Hell*? "I know," said Rodin, "that at this moment man is suffering." Is this the suffering depicted in the panels of his infernal gate? Is it the suffering of Rodin's own times, which did not differ greatly from that of today? Is the hell which his Dantesque gate portrays not that of his century and ours? Is not *The Thinker* pondering on the events of his day and ours? The hungry figure of Ugolino devouring his children is not only a revival of the myth of Chronos in the "Divine Comedy." It is a hideous image of a hideous and as yet unresolved problem — that of world starvation.

The Martyr, another character portrayed on the gate, is also still topical; we cannot boast that martyrs are extinct on our planet. In classical mythology Danaid *(see page 23)* was one of a group of fifty sisters condemned eternally to refill a barrel which emptied again as soon as it was full. According to mythologists, she represented irrigation, which requires endless repetition of the same labor. Perhaps labor is the keyword. Before creating *The Gates*, writes Jean Selz, Rodin had conceived the idea of a monument which at first glance had no connection with that which the French government was later

Eternal Spring, 1884. Bronze, h. 25⅜″ (64.4 cm). Musée Rodin, Paris

VICTOR HUGO, 1916-1918. Marble, h. 26¼″ (65.7 cm). Musée Rodin, Paris

Alphonse Legros, 1881-1882.   Bronze, h. 12⁹⁄₁₆″ (32 cm).   Musée Rodin, Paris

to commission and which caused him to give up his first idea. But did he entirely abandon it? Can one not see traces of it in *The Gates of Hell*? *The Thinker*'s muscles make him either an athlete or a manual laborer. Maybe he is just an unskilled worker or a farm-hand. If he has sat down to think, it is because he is accustomed to stand, and meditation is an unusual exercise for him. What is he thinking about? Might not the subject of his sombre thoughts be the poverty of the working classes in Rodin's day? The "wretched of the earth, the prisoners of starvation," as they are called in "The Internationale," might they not be symbolized by the tortured throng which populates the panels of the Dantesque door? Rodin was nine when Karl Marx wrote his "Eighteenth Brumaire of Napoleon Bonaparte." He lived through attempted assassinations by anarchists and the growth of the Socialist movement. He became internationally famous at a time when the voice of Jean Jaurès could be heard. Did he hear it? Great creative artists cannot stand entirely aside from the major movements in the society to which they belong. He died in the year of the Bolshevik Revolution in Russia, and its triumph was also in a way his triumph, since the monument which he tought of putting up was to be dedicated to the glory of labor. Thus *The Thinker* — who officially is also *The Poet* — would be in fact a manual laborer, a man of physical work, thinking about how to escape from oppression and already beginning to succeed. He sits, like a whole series of Michelangelo's people who also belong in the realm of thought, such as the sculpted Moses on the tomb of Julius II and the Lorenzo II de Medici, also called *The Thinker*, or the paintings of the prophets Jeremiah and Isaiah in the frescoes of the Sistine Chapel. The Michelangelo character who most closely resembles Rodin's *Thinker* is, however, to be found in the famous *Last Judgment* painted on the end wall of the Sistine Chapel, which is nearer to Rodin's *Gates of Hell* than any other work of the past. This character sits in the same strange and surprising attitude as Rodin's contemplative athlete, with his right elbow on his left thigh — an attitude which makes one think of yoga in connection with his mental exercice. But in Rodin's work this posture plays a significant role: the right arm of this intellectually endowed Hercules points to one wing of the *Gates* and his left arm to the other. In view of this function which he fulfils, his role is clearly an important one. In his *Last Judgment* Michelangelo's character is a damned soul lost in a crowd of his fellows. Rodin gave his wretch the position Michelangelo gave to Christ. In other words it is the Christian world (or at least a certain conception of it) which suffers decapitation in the same way as *The Walking Man*. If head and heaven are synonymous, the head being the summit of the body, as the heavens are the head of the universe, one could even say that the ruling class is another equivalent of heaven or head. Rodin, therefore, by singling out his condemned soul, reverses the social order and announces the liberation of the working classes whose fate hangs no longer on the heavens but on themselves.

THE HAND OF GOD, 1898.   Marble, h. 29″ (73.7 cm)
The Metropolitan Museum of Art, New York. Gift of Edward D. Adams

THOUGHT, 1893-1895.   Marble, h. 29¼″ (74.2 cm).   Musée d'Orsay, Paris

Mozart (Portrait of Gustav Mahler), 1911. Marble, h. 20″ (50.9 cm). Musée Rodin, Paris

MADAME MORLA VICUÑA, 1888.   Marble, h. 22⅜″ (56.9 cm).   Musée d'Orsay, Paris

Jean-Paul Sartre reproached the Impressionists for the optimism of the light colors they were using at a moment of tragedy for the working classes. He could not reproach Rodin in the same way, for Rodin is creating not paradise, but a society still in its infernal stage. In any case, inspired as he was by Michelangelo, why did he chose to speak through Dante, instead of in his own name? And if this intermediary was forced on him, why did he accept it with enthusiasm? The choice of hell as a theme was itself significant. Dante wrote his "Paradise," but Rodin did not portray it. In other words, as with *The Walking Man*, the "Divine Comedy" has been decapitated; from the very beginning, heaven was to be omitted.

THE EMBRACE (TWO FIGURES), c. 1905. Pencil, watercolor, and gouache, 12¾″ × 9⅞″ (32.5 × 25.1 cm)
The Metroplitan Museum of Art, New York. Kennedy Fund

"Butcher!" the voice in the rotunda in 1900 had shouted. Rodin was indeed a butcher, more so than his anonymous accuser perhaps realized. If one compares the uproar over *The Walking Man* in 1900 with that over *Balzac* in 1898, one can see why. In these two works — these two crimes, one might say — Rodin has accomplished thorough destruction. Combining the two statues would give one complete man — a walking man with Balzac's head. Rodin had tried this solution with his naked *Balzac*, and rejected it. The definitive *Balzac* is a head set on a rock, in other words a head without a body. If one adds together the negative elements of the two, the headless giant and the bodiless head, one has a man without either head or body. In other words, man, at least classical man, has been destroyed. Very possibly this was in Rodin's mind when he created the theme of *The Gates of Hell*. In replacing Michelangelo's God by a condemned man, and the prince, or the social class which claimed that its power was God-given, by a workman who draws his strenght from the earth, Rodin has destroyed the classical conception of the universe and of society. But in order to produce grand pieces where social and artistic classicism itself was to be destroyed, Rodin had to act with the authority born of a full knowledge of the facts (another reason for his enthusiastic acceptance of Dante's theme). He himself therefore had to be a classic, an illustrator or a descendant of the classics, like Dante or Michelangelo. How did he become the classical butcher of classicism? The story starts in 1875.

MEDITATION ON MOSES

In that year, an energetic-looking Frenchman with knitted brows arrived in Rome from Brussels, where he had been engaged in ornamental sculpture. He walked into the church of San Pietro in Vincoli and advanced purposefully toward the tomb of Julius II. In the center of the base of this marble monument was carved Michelangelo's *Moses*. What secrets did Michelangelo trasmit to Rodin? Now that their work can be judged in its entirety, one can affirm that not only did these two artists unite in depicting *The Thinker* and great cosmosociological scenes such as *The Last Judgment* and *The Gates of Hell*, but they also shared a taste for strength and certain muscular exaggerations. The muscles in the necks of *The Shades*, and of *The Night* on the tomb of Giuliano II de Medici in Florence, are the same. Mutilation and decapitation are not inventions of Rodin's, but can also be found in Michelangelo — a sketch for the Medici Madonna is headless, and one arm of the finished statue is so hidden in drapery that from some angles it seems to be missing altogether. If Rodin's unfinished sculptures are famous, Michelangelo's are equally so. The head of *The Day* on the same tomb in Florence is barely roughed in, while in his marble entitled *Dawn* Rodin reversed this idea by finishing the head but losing the rest of the body in the stone.

Michelangelo's sensuality is expressed in his love of nakedness. (He left all the characters in his *Last Judgment* unclothed, but the modesty of the time made another artist, Daniel de Volterra, cover them with drapery). Rodin did not suffer this misfortune, but he was no less sensual. Men thought he looked like Jove, but women said he had the appeal of a satyr. Some of his statues rank among the most erotic in existence: his famous couple entitled *The Kiss (see page 32)* is typical. The same sensuality is to be found in *Eternal Spring (see page 49)*, *The Metamorphoses of Ovid (see page 20)*, and *I Am Beautiful (see page 18)*, which are just random examples. Ancient sculptors fell in love with their works and, if the story of Pygmalion and Galatea inspired Rodin *(see page 40)*, it was because he hardly distinguished between an artistic creation and the physical act. During the last seventeen years of the life of the "Master of Meudon" (so called after his villa outside Paris), an Austrian doctor was fighting the same battle as he, to rehabilitate sex in an era still choked with prudery and hypocrisy. Sigmund Freud met with the same violent opposition as Rodin. Like Freud, Rodin was introducing a new man, and to do so, to anticipate him — that is, to herald his appearance — he had to mutilate and smash the classical body he so adored. A tragic fate, but Rodin was not the first to suffer thus; Michelangelo had prophesied the same superman — or at least the same metamorphosed humanity — more than three centuries before anyone dared to create his image.

Did the visitor with the knitted brows ponder all this before Michelangelo's *Moses* in the church of San Pietro in Vincoli? Perhaps without realizing its full import, he sensed a strange affinity, like that of Delacroix with Rubens, or Cézanne with El Greco. Great innovators need illustrious forerunners both to support them in their daring and to temper their defiance by the mellowing effect of distance. Rodin's celebrated forerunner was always the creator of *Moses*, as Cézanne's was the Cretan who went to live and die at Toledo. Cézanne felt a bond between himself and Rodin. The story is told of how one day they met at Monet's house, when the man who had said of himself, "A painter like me appears only once in three centuries," threw himself on his knees before the Olympian-headed sculptor who deserved as much as did Puget the epithet of the French Michelangelo and cried "You, at least, have been successful!" In fact, both were equally successful, though Cézanne's succes, his real succes, which he himself never knew in his lifetime but is so self-evident to us, was the fact that modern painting would be inconceivable without him. Likewise, the true success of Rodin was not his material achievement (which afforded him his many studios and assistants) but that new school of sculpture to which his work gave birth. El Greco and Michelangelo had not had such success, neither of them having anyone to carry on his work. Seen in this light, in the same way that Cézanne is a successful El Greco, Rodin is not only the French Michelangelo but also the Italian's historical heir.

STUDY OF A NUDE, n.d.   Pencil, watercolor and gouache, 12¾″ × 9⅝″ (32.5 × 24.5 cm)
Musée Rodin, Paris

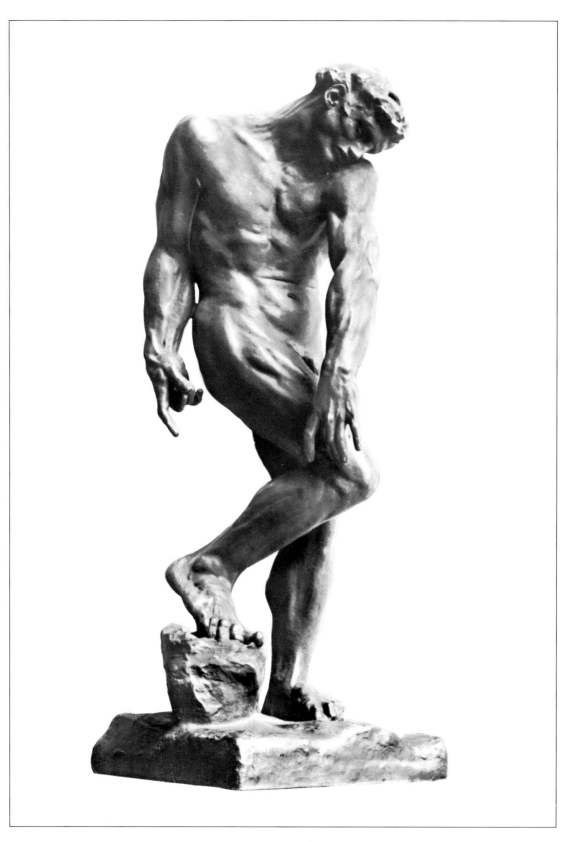

ADAM, c. 1881.   Bronze, h. 78″ (198 cm)
The Art Institute, Chicago. Collection Mrs. Harold T. Martin

EVE AFTER THE FALL, 1886.   Marble, h. 11¹³⁄₁₆″ (30 cm)
The Art Institute, Chicago. Collection Mr. and Mrs. Martin A. Ryerson

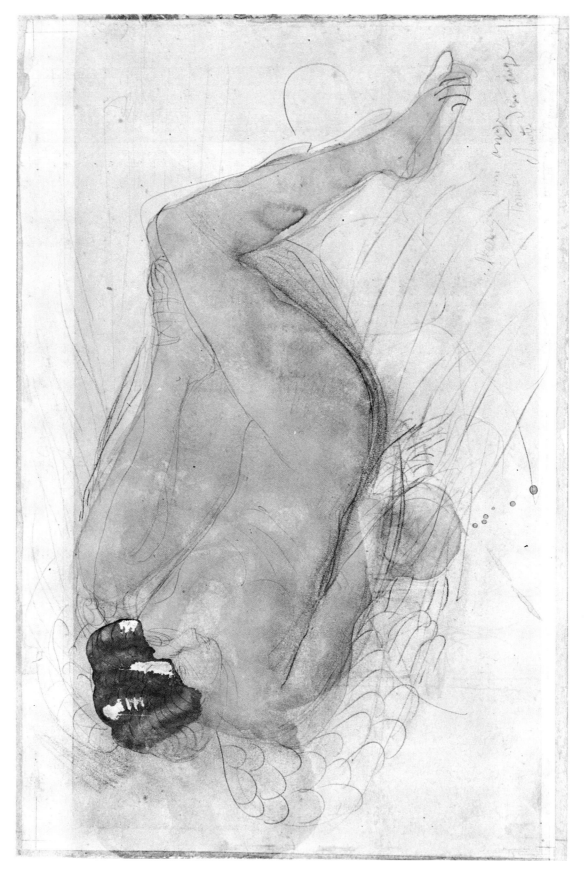

Fallen Angel, n.d.   Pencil and watercolor, 12⅜″ × 19½″ (31.5 × 49.5 cm).   Musée Bourdelle, Paris

In the church of San Pietro in Vincoli in 1875, did the vigorous-looking visitor already realize that he was to give the creator of Julius II's tomb the chance of which history had deprived him, because in the sixteenth century people were not ready to look properly at his visual offerings? Rodin must have had some vague foreboding, but his dominant thought must have been that in order to have the influence and spiritual descendants which the famous Florentine lacked, he must first become as great a sculptor as he. Hence his passionate interest in *Moses*. But why is his attention directed more particularly at his beard? Perhaps because he envied it or because he sensed that he might one day have an equally luxuriant growth, or else because he noticed a gesture of the right hand of the Law-Giver which deflected its flow, so that there is a depression at the level of his stomach which carves out a hollow in his thorax. This concave form he adopted and used, notably in his *Eustache de Saint-Pierre*. But at that moment he had not yet thought of the group of *The Burghers of Calais*, which was the precursor of Etienne Martin's *Dwellings*, and only entered his life nine years later. Rather, he was remembering the long hours of study of classical works in the Louvre. The ancients did not hollow out their figures, but made them bulge. He also remembered the medieval statuary he had studied at Rheims during his journey. Like Michelangelo and unlike the ancient sculptors, medieval artists made concave figures with corbel-like silhouettes. All at once his face lit up. He had found what he was looking for. Michelangelo was not what one supposed him to be, the continuer of classical art, but "the last and greatest of the Gothics,", as Rodin was to confide much later to Paul Gsell — a fact which had escaped everyone before him. Thus he who understood the great Florentine so well would perhaps be able to equal him and across the span of the centuries which divided them become his sole spiritual heir and the sole worthy successor of his art. It was probably at this moment of exaltation that he conceived the idea of a sculpture whose strange destiny and metamorphoses were to resemble a self-portrait and the symbol of his role in the evolution of Western art and thought. This takes us back to Brussels, two years later.

THE CONTROVERSY OVER THE CASTING

The scene took place in January 1877 at the Exhibition of the Cercle Artistique of Brussels, where discussion centered around a plaster sculpture, *The Vanquished*, by a young artist newly returned from Italy. Primarily this was the figure of a shepherd (Moses had originally been a shepherd). Perhaps this was Rodin's way of approaching Michelangelo's suject, but modifying it — his Moses was young — while remaining within the same realm, for *The Vanquished* is also a memorial to those *Slaves* which the great Florentine regarded as allegories of the cities conquered by Pope Julius II.

How did Rodin's *Vanquished* come to be a peaceful keeper of sheep? By the removal of the staff which the young peasant held in his right hand to lean on (a much less serious mutilation than those which were to follow), so that he is disarmed, like a conquered soldier. This was not, however, the subject of discussion at the Cercle Artistique. Opinions were divided, some people saying that it was a wonderful, vivid piece of sculpture, while others maintained that this was hardly surprising, since it was a cast, meaning that Rodin had contented himself with performing a number of operations which were in no way creative, posing a nude youth and taking a cast of his entire body. On this suspicion burst the controversy over *The Vanquished*, which was to become the controversy over *The Age of Bronze*, when the same statue was exhibited in Paris with the new title a few months later.

Was Rodin guilty? Even if the suspicions of the people in Brussels and Paris in 1877 were well-founded, we would not use this term today, because casting has become respectable. Picasso, the American George Segal, the Frenchman Ipoustéguy and many others have used this process. Nearer to Rodin, between 1910 and 1926, Gaudi introduced castings for the figures of saints and apostles in his decoration of the Sagrada Familia at Barcelona. So Rodin's accusers were actually making an innovator of him, but he defended himself fiercely against their attacks, because he had other ways of surrendering to nature, through a creative use of improvisation and chance.

At the Hôtel Biron in Paris, which became the Rodin Museum, Auguste Rodin used to observe and wait, occasionally making a rapid sketch of one of his famous drawings, recording the gestures of one of the nude models circulating freely in front of him. At this moment no-one had yet heard of improvised music, Max Ernst had not applied his "frottages" and the "Tachistes" had not yet perfected their spontaneous painting. However, in the relationship of artist and model, unlike the other contemporary sculptors, who posed their models in deliberately contrived and lengthily ponderous attitudes, Rodin was already using the technique of laissez-faire and improvisation. When the little girl asked him in 1900 why his walking man had no head, he could have replied, "Because the head, which is the seat of reason and will, is no longer enough to grasp beauty." This leads me to refer to another walking man. Unlike the giant at the World Fair, he was normally equipped with a head and two arms. Rodin conceived and executed him at the same time as *The Age of Bronze*. Unfortunately, according to some historians, the artistic world has lost track of him. One can easily guess his name. He was a man in the Bible who was to Moses what Rodin wanted to be to Michelangelo — a great successor. In the last three verses of Alfred de Vigny's poem "Moïse" this great successor "pensif et pâlissant" ("thoughtful and pale") led the Hebrew people toward the Promised Land which he was to conquer. Joshua. The

CAMBODIAN WOMAN, SEATED, 1906.
Graphite, pen and ink with watercolor and gouache, 12⅜″ × 7¾″ (31.3 × 19.8 cm)
Musée Rodin, Paris

poet described him as "walking." How did Rodin express this idea of movement? The answer was to be found in the rotunda in 1900, in full view of the public. It is the metal giant of whom the little girl, the daughter of an art critic, asked why he had no head. Rodin smilingly replied, "Because he's walking" and went on to explain, "If he had a head, that's all you'd see." Rodin was well aware of the importance of the head, and was ready to yield to it. From 1900 on, apart from the changes made to *The Gates of Hell*, some nude sculptures and a few monuments which revived old themes without much alteration, his main production consisted of a splendid series of portraits reduced to heads and their immediate surroundings. Heads exercise a sway over one's eyes both because they are the seat of the intelligence on which men pride themselves, and also because they are the best-known part of the body, since they are always open to view. The other parts of the body seem by comparison abstract, or extremely ambiguous. Thus, by decapitating his giant, Rodin also introduced abstract sculpture.

It is by people's heads that one distinguishes them most surely from each other and heads are therefore not suitable for portraying vague reveries. Nevertheless in his marble sculptures, especially *Puvis de Chavannes, Mozart (see page 55)* and one of his portraits of *Victor Hugo (see page 50)*, Rodin often tried to take up the challenge and create a head as hazy and evanescent as a slippery chute down which one falls in a dream. Conversely, by indicating and even exaggerating the characteristics of the other parts of the body, he treated them like features, and even spoke of the smile of a trunk or a belly. But the best way to make a trunk or a belly smile or grimace, or to make them attractive like faces, is to omit their chief rival, the real face. This is why *The Walking Man* has no head and why, among other reasons, Rodin once said, "His head is everywhere," when someone asked him the same question as the little girl. This translation of the head into the body and the legs makes a monster as disturbing as the monsters of Picasso and very similar to those created by Miró and Enrico Baj, which consist of a head resting on two hands. But to the little girl, even though she was the daughter of an art critic, the bronze giant was headless. Rodin said this was because he was walking; in other words, to make one look at his legs. But his legs are motionless. How do they convey this impression of walking which Joshua must convey if he is to look like a leader? Rodin did not explain this to the little girl but to an adult who was making a collection of his sayings. As Jean Selz pointed out, *The Walking Man*'s left leg is longer than his right. However, to comply with the rules of anatomy and the movement of walking, the left heel should be raised off the ground, but is in fact as firmly attached to the plinth as its companion. Rodin explained to Paul Gsell that this was because he had combined many different positions in one — the position with the heel raised and that when the heel touches the ground. Rodin has thus made in

WOMAN IN BLUE, n.d.   Pencil and watercolor wash, 19⁹⁄₁₆″ × 9⅝″ (32 × 24 c.5 cm).   Musée Bourdelle, Paris

this leg what Picasso, Braque and the Cubists made in those faces which closely unite front-view and profile. He has displayed simultaneously two views of an object which can only be seen in succession, and this was not in 1907, the year when Cubism was born, but in 1877, exactly thirty years earlier. So Rodin is a prophet of Cubism, of Futurism, of the new man who was to rise from the ashes of the old man. He thus seems to be more a St. John the Baptist than a Moses or a Joshua. When one considers all that his art foretold, one should perhaps look for his portrait in the face of the Messenger of Christ rather than in that of the Conqueror of the Promised Land, for these two characters are closely linked.

THE CONQUEROR OF THE PROMISED LAND

It is worth studying the genealogy of *St. John the Baptist Preaching* — its full title — within Rodin's work. It was carved in 1877, one year after *The Age of Bronze*, exhibited at the Salon in 1880 and awarded Third Prize. It was intended to be the son of *The Walking Man*, who was a preliminary study for it (but was not shown to the public until twenty years later). Who was the father of the headless man and the grandfather of the Messenger of Christ? Madame Cécile Goldscheider has suggested an answer that shows how Rodin practiced the technique of improvisation; it may be found in the following anecdote, which dates from 1877.

The young sculptor who had caused an uproar when he exhibited *The Vanquished*, that conquered man who was a shepherd and subsequently became *Man Awakening to Nature* and, finally, *The Age of Bronze*, was at the time in Paris, supervising the unpacking of some sculptures which had just arrived from Brussels. He gave a sigh of relief when he saw that *The Age of Bronze* was intact, but unfortunately not all the statues were undamaged. Was it a jolt in the train, clumsy handling or bad packing that had damaged *Joshua* so badly? The trunk was broken in two places, at the stomach and and the bottom of the belly, displaying cracks similar to those in *Male Torso* at the Petit-Palais and in the body of *The Walking Man*. The lower limbs were broken at the top of the thighs. These breaks are as clearly visible in the latter in good condition, but only one thigh of the former. The two sculptures are probably cast from the same fragments of Joshua, though one of them — the walker — comprises more than the other. Both are headless and armless.

"Butcher," the unknown voice had cried. Rodin might have replied, "I'm not the butcher, it was the train, it was the shippers, it was fate." We know he was a fatalist, but the result in this case is a monster. In 1877 Rodin made a statue of a superbly

ETERNAL SPRING, 1885.   Marble, h. 28″ (71 cm)
The Metropolitan Museum of Art, New York. Bequest of Isaac D. Fletcher

THE WEEPING LION, 1881.   Marble, h. 11″ (28 cm).   Musée Rodin, Paris

beautiful young man.   How could he accept this monstrous image of a body supported on two legs?   The answer is simply that for him all nature — including monsters, which like luck and fate are part of nature — was beautiful.   He said repeatedly to Paul Gsell, "In nature everything is beautiful, everything."   Even pain, even hell (this was one reason for his sculpting *The Gates of Hell*), even execution and amputation, even pathetic old age as in *She Who Was the Helmet-Maker's Once Beautiful Wife*.   This truth, if such it is, he shows in both its aspects.   Beauty is that which looks beautiful *(The Age of Bronze)* and also that which looks ugly (the humiliated old woman who in her triumphant youth had been celebrated by Villon).   Rodin extolled everything, old age and youth alike, and found not a fraction of an inch in the universe which was not supremely beautiful.   This discovery bordered on wisdom, and so, at the age of sixty, holding the hand of a little girl who had asked him a difficult and even agonizing question, he retained his expression of Olympian serenity, even though he could not repress a muscular contraction in his fingers.   Simple intellectual honesty compelled him, however, to acknowledge that this reconciliation with the universe was a difficult task.   Very well, let us admit that ugliness, like evil and wrong, does not exist, as certain philosophers have maintained; even so, there is an aspect of ugliness which obsesses us and from which we can hardly tear ourselves away.   How can one remove it?   Rodin's answer was in the capacity to perceive.   "It is not that there is not beauty for our eyes to see," he said to Gsell, "but that our eyes cannot see the beauty there is."

The best artist is he who best sees this beauty and best transmits his vision to others, that is, he who has the best eyes and the best hands.   Hence the importance of hands in Rodin's work.   He can on occasion regard a single hand moulded into tiny human bodies — *The Hand of God (see page 53)* — as a complete sculpture.   His *Burghers of Calais* have huge, strongly expressive hands which seem to speak.   The hand on which *The Thinker* rests his massive head is also enormous.   This is probably because hands, like faces, are most often visible in everyday life.   We know them well, can interpret their movements, or at least most of their movements, and this knowledge and the attention we pay them magnify them in our eyes.   Hands are also skilled, as is *The Thinker*'s hand; they are the buttress and necessary complement to thought.   Thanks to his hands the sculptor can express his vision and his widsom.

St. John the Baptist talks with his fingers as much as with his mouth and even with his whole body.   He walks like *The Walking Man* and is thus a prophet: to foretell the future, it is enough to walk when all the world stands still.   And the future he foretells is the future of Joshua, the conquest of the Promised Land, that is, a place where men are not alone, where they wander no longer in the wilderness, where they are reconciled to the world.   *Balzac* is equally expressive.   He is a head poised, to use Miró's phrase,

NUDE WITH FOLDED ARMS, n.d.   Pencil and watercolor wash, 12⁹⁄₁₆″ × 8⁷⁄₈″ (32 × 22,5 cm)
Musée Bourdelle, Paris

CAMBODIAN DANCER, n.d.
Graphite, pen and ink with watercolor and gouache, 12⅛″ × 9⅝″ (30.6 × 24.5 cm)
Musée Rodin, Paris

SHE WHO WAS THE HELMET-MAKER'S ONCE BEAUTIFUL WIFE, before 1885.   Bronze, h. 19¹¹⁄₁₆″ (50 cm)
Musée Rodin, Paris

"on a mountain." He is a man whose body has become a montain, a head finally reconciled to the world, for it harmonizes perfectly with the mountain of the world. How this head became reconciled to the world, *The Walking Man* can teach us: by losing itself. The world has taken its place. This probably was what Rodin was trying to say when he replied, "But his head is everywhere." So *The Walking Man* walks to the rhythm of the universe.

Still the question remains unanswered as to how one reaches such great results and such a formidable reconciliation, how such an arduously wrought peace treaty came to be signed. Rodin replied that this reconciliation is in the eyes of the beholder and that the world became receptive to a certain vision, the vision expressed by his works. But again, the question arises as to what this potent method of perception actually is. One day, as I looked at *The Thinker*, I realized that the method of perception to which Rodin's work bears witness is that of a colorist. The common denominator to which Rodin reduces everything he sees, to unify it and stamp it with beauty, is a living volume which in the three-dimensional world of sculpture is the equivalent of living color in the two-dimensional world of painting. Both have the same enemy: the demands of clear contour, or in current artistic terminology, "line," which is very fragile because it is demanding. The slightest nuance of color, the least vibration of volume, upsets it and consequently destroys it, because its definition is clarity. Therefore not all who see vivid volume and color succeed in grasping contour. Cézanne, who saw color, said, "Contour escapes me." Looking at *The Thinker* and seeing its living volume, I had exactly the same impression. When I thought I had grasped a line, it escaped from me almost as quickly, because I could not determine its whereabouts or discover what kind of straight line or curve it was. It wavered, slipped and vanished. Of course, one can make very beautiful works with clear lines; in that case volume and line are only the means to obtain this contour, which kills them or at best reduces them to a subordinate role. Even if I had not perceived Rodin's colorism when looking at *The Thinker*, I would often have been made aware of it. In Rodin's art collection, beside ancient sculptures such as a Roman marble representing Agrippina or the marble copy of Praxitele's *Satyr*, can be found a painting far ahead of its time which betrays a bold decision. It is a canvas by a great colorist, Van Gogh's *Portrait of Mr. Tanguy*.

Rodin had been a painter; his watercolors herald the style of Matisse and Dufy, two other great colorists. His pictures painted in Belgium are probably nearer to the style of Corot, the "valoriste," but at that time coloring sculptures by making volumes move concerned him more than coloring canvas. Besides, he was still seeking his way. Later, when this search was ended, he was to explain most precisely to Paul Gsell, who devoted a whole chapter of his memoirs to this subject, how sculpture could be colored without

CAMBODIAN DANCER, 1906
Graphite, pen and ink with watercolor and gouache, 12¼″ × 7⅝″ (31.2 × 19.5 cm)
Musée Rodin, Paris

CAMBODIAN DANCER, 1906
Graphite, pen and ink with watercolor and gouache, 11¾″ × 7¾″ (30 × 19.7 cm)
Musée Rodin, Paris

THE IDYLL OF IXELLES, 1876.   Bronze, h. 20⅝″ (52.5 cm).   Musée Rodin, Paris

color by an intense manipulation of the material, so that holes, cuts, scratches, lashes, curlings, crumplings, wounds, and scars were not just manifestations of sadism but also the means of giving life and evidence of love for the effect of color through volume. This love of color showed itself early in his life, for around 1855 visitors to the Louvre could see in the rooms of the great Venetian colorists a boy of about fifteen displaying simultaneously admiration, a wish to shout (at least to himself) "I am a painter, too," and despair, for the paints needed to reproduce these lovely colors of the Venetian school were expensive, too expensive for the impecunious young man. Later, the same visitors saw him again, this time with paper and pencil or charcoal — cheaper materials — copying the old masters. "I acquired a taste for it," Rodin recalled, "and that is how I became a sculptor." But he was still a colorist, that is, a man whom the contours of things eluded.

His vanishing contours, betrayed by their sinuousness and the breaks in their lines, embody the risk of the dissolution of form, and because he ran this risk Rodin has been compared to the Impressionists, who found themselves in the same situation as he, and can be regarded as a forerunner of the informal artist. However, Rodin warded off the threat of dissolution, and his tactics are very similar to those of Van Gogh, in whose works form is retained by a kind of life current which creates huge eddies. In Rodin this function is fulfilled by the gestures of his figures, gestures so striking and emphatic that they seem like letters of the alphabet, printed characters or simple geometric figures. The square and its diagonal, formed by shoulders and arms, are seen in *Eve (see page 63)*. A square encloses *The Three Shades*, whose arms are threefold radia. *The Thinker* seen from the three-quarter position consists of a zigzag in a semicircle. The right arm of *St. John the Baptist* forms a capital V, while the outside extremity of his body and the curve of his left arm form a capital D. *The Prodigal Son (see page 34)* is a capital C backwards. The back of the bronze woman in the Rodin Museum, who also symbolizes despair, forms a capital C joined to a capital K on its back, made by her arms and legs *(see page 44)*. The twisting of the unmutilated *Meditation (see page 19)* creates a long-handled sickle or a capital M. In *I Am Beautiful (see page 18)* there is a capital C reversed and crowned with an N on its side. A capital T askew can be seen in *The Weeping Lion (see page 72)* and a capital C in its mouth. There is another capital T askew and a reversed Z embracing the bronze version of *Eternal Spring (see page 49)*. A small x with two detached curves contains the marble version of the same subject *(see page 71)*, in the lower part of which one can see the lines converge. Finally, there is the inverted Y of the large *Walking Man*. Why has he no head or arms? Rodin might have replied, "Precisely in order to make this clear, inverted Y."

CARYATID (CROUCHING WOMAN), 1886. Marble, h. 17¾″ (45 cm)
Museum of Fine Arts, Boston. Gift of Julia Isham Taylor

THE FALLEN CARYATID CARRYING HER STONE, c. 1891.   Bronze, h. 17½″ (44.5 cm)
The Art Institute, Chicago. Gift of Robert Allerton

CAMBODIAN DANCER, 1906
Graphite, pen and ink with watercolor and gouache, 12¼″ × 7¾″ (31.2 × 19.7 cm)
Musée Rodin, Paris

THE WALK TO THE STARS

This is the story of a noise, the noise of the rustling of dead leaves heard by men of a far-off age when everyone went naked. It is night, and a fire is burning in the forest. The rustling of the leaves draws nearer, when all at once a cry is heard. Into the circle of light bursts a headless, armless monster. Another step and he becomes normal, as the light falls on his face and upper limbs. To the question about his giant's lack of face and arms, Rodin might have replied, "Because I admire Rembrandt, who decapitates and mutilates his subjects too, by plunging their heads or limbs or both into a deep, dense and secret darkness." From this point of view, that of the chiaroscuro, Rodin's mutilated creations provide the imagination with an impression of darkness: volume is light, and everything outside that compact volume is shadow. One receives the same impression, and for similar reasons, from a number of modern works which I would describe as "torn." This secretion of shadow, comparable to an octopus's secretion of ink, has the notable advantage of isolating sculpture from its surroundings and protecting it, in the same way as the octopus protects itself with its inky effusions. It gives sculpture its independence in relation to its surroundings and especially to architecture.

Rodin must have felt a certain satisfaction. He had long been engaged in producing pot-boilers, however accomplished, and even after the scandal of *The Age of Bronze*, which made him famous, he accepted a job in the Sèvres porcelain works, where until 1882 he designed vases and cups *(see page 92)* and decorated them himself. His hardest moment was during his stay in Belgium, when he was doing decorative work subject to the requirements of architecture. He must have found it pleasant, a sort of revenge, to liberate the sculptor from the tyranny of the architect. But this is only one aspect of the secretion of darkness. There is another, which is perhaps even more impressive and stems from the fact that it is not only produced by mutilation. The pliant forms resulting from Rodin's colorism, even in the figures of adults, subtly suggest a soft foetus living in the darkness of the womb. The same idea of dark, prenatal life is conjured up very precisely in *The Fish-Woman*, because the foetus within the womb is like a fish in its liquid habitat, but also in a more general sense by the bracket or the cave form (to be taken up by Pevsner), the cave being another symbol of the womb. Again one sees this similarity to the foetus in his curled-up people, such as *Danaid (see pages 22 and 23)* or the woman in the group entitled *I Am Beautiful* — an obeisance to Charles Baudelaire. The woman is being held up in the air by the hands of an athletic lover *(see page 18)*. The foetus is a passenger too. Those of his sculptures and marbles that were left deliberately unfinished demostrate equally the theme of gestation, and in this context, in spite of their whiteness, secrete darkness, a darkness sometimes intensified by the difficulty of interpretation, as in *Ariane* (where are her head and her arm?). But

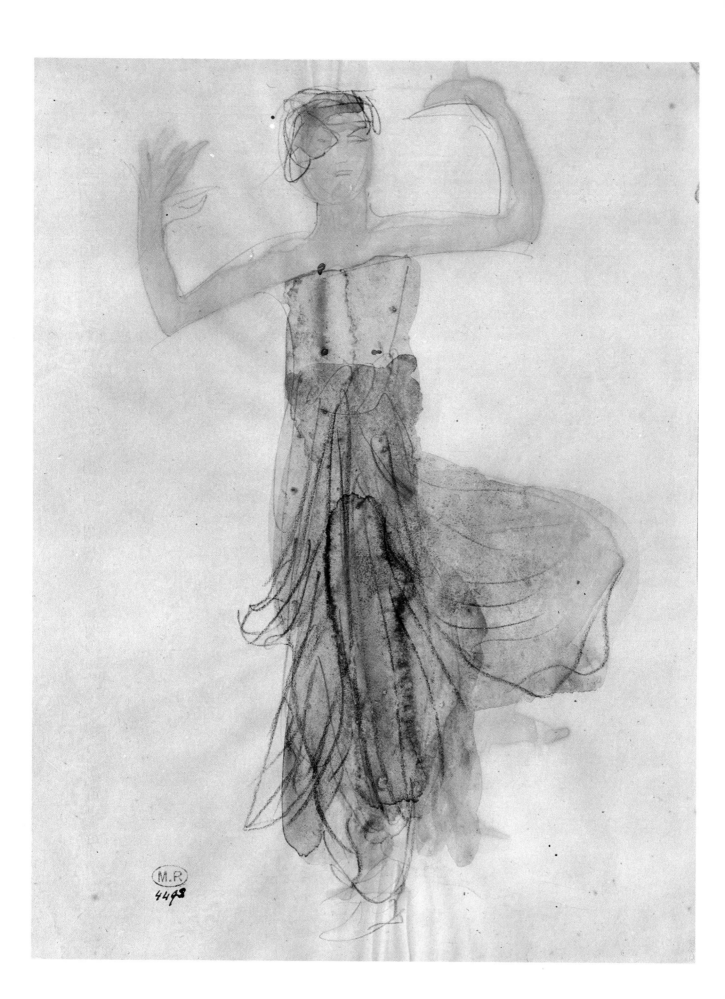

GROUP OF CAMBODIAN DANCERS, 1906
Pen, brown ink with watercolor and gouache
11⅜″ × 11″ (28.7 × 27.8 cm)
Musée Rodin, Paris

◁

CAMBODIAN DANCER, 1906
Graphite, pen and brown ink with watercolor and gouache
12⅝″ × 9½″ (32.2 × 24.1 cm)
Musée Rodin, Paris

the gestation suggested by these sculptures is either that inverse gestation which puts an end to life and decomposes it into mineral form, thereby confirming the idea of darkness, or else the gestation which is birth. Birth is, however, a state near to that of uterine darkness, so that the shadows never wholly disperse. The same ambiguity, with the same result, is to be found in the amputation when considered from this point of view. They may symbolize castration, which is a kind of death and thus night, but they may also symbolize the cutting of the umbilical cord, that is, the arrival into the world and the achievement of independence. But this is also called birth and, though largely a matter of light, does not wholly dispel the shadows.

Did the mutilations of *The Walking Man* symbolize castration, the death of an old world, the world of craftsmanship, for instance, whose passing Rodin regretted as much as he distrusted the rise of industry, saying as he walked in front of a factory from which issued a deafening clatter of machinery, "Great forests grow, but make less noise?" Or are these missing parts positive symbols of birth? Rodin's realism was too deep for one to be sure, but this would not have been a wholly optimistic solution. However, he certainly foresaw the arrival of a new man, and in spite of his adherence to classicism he guessed that this man would not be a classical man, for though he pretended to rely on heaven he was in fact only interested in himself. By adding together the missing head of the bronze giant and *Balzac*'s missing body, one arrived at the knife without blade or handle which André Breton, quoting Lichtenberg, used to define as black humor. Rodin's black humor! What did it consist of, once classical man was gone? Rilke has given a beautifully worded answer. First he speaks of *The Age of Bronze*, which he sees as enveloped in a closed space, a sort of prenatal space in which the adolescent is still imprisoned, as in his mother's womb; then the figure of *St. John the Baptist*, whose gestures widen and dilate the space around him, and finally, several mutilated statues, including *The Walking Man*; in this case the suggested space is so dilated that it seems to reach the stars. Rodin can therefore be said to have eliminated heaven and replace it with another, a new heaven where man would no longer project his image but rather himself into that space; a heaven on which man no longer depended but with which he harmonized. So *The Walking Man* whose "head is everywhere" is the walk to the stars, heralding the fantastic pyrotechnics and the discovery of the planets, like so many other "Promised Lands," which we are beginning to witness. Classical man, this man whose sad reign extended well beyong the classical era, the man who withdrew from the world, thus turning it into a desert and spreading around him endless reproductions of himself, like an opaque screen, is dead, like Nietzche's God. What remains of him? As Rilke suggested, more remains than has been destroyed. The world remains, an enlarged world, and a new, more lucid man with a deeper or more complex idea of the divine, more able to penetrate the great forces of nature, where, as Rodin said, provided one can see it, "Everything is beautiful."

BALZAC, 1893-1897.   Bronze, h. 106¼″ (270 cm).   Musée Rodin, Paris

THE CATHEDRAL, 1908. Stone, h. 25³⁄₁₆″ (64 cm). Musée Rodin, Paris

BIOGRAPHY

1840   On November 12, François Auguste René Rodin was born in Paris. His father was a police official. Rodin was a bad pupil until he entered the Decorative Arts High School, where from 1854 to 1857 he studied, drawing from memory under Lecoq de Boisbaudran. Took courses in literature and history at the Collège de France. Showed admiration for Dante. Earned his living from decorative art and designs for cabinet-work and jewelry.

1860   First portraits, his father Jean-Baptiste.

1862   Death of his sister Maria, aged 22. Despair. Entered a religious order.

1863   Portrait of Father Pierre-Julien Eymard, who sent him home, saying he had more talent for sculpture than for the religious life.

1864   An old porter he met in the street served as model for his *Man with the Broken Nose*, his first original work. Formed a liaison with a seamstress, Marie-Rose Beuret, who bore him a son in 1866 and remained his life-long companion. Worked for a mediocre sculptor, Carrier-Belleuse, until 1870.

1870   Enlisted in the National Guard. Discharged on account of shortsightedness.

1872   Temporary estrangement from Carrier-Belleuse. Remained in Brussels, though penniless and starving. Completed a bust of *Man with the Broken Nose*.

1873   February 12. Contract with Van Rasbourg, whereby this competent but unimaginative sculptor was to take credit for Rodin's works produced in Belgium.

1875   Traveled to Italy via Rheims, Pontarlier, Lausanne, Geneva and Mont-Cenis. In Italy visited Turin, Genoa (where he saw works of Puget, the "French Michelangelo"), Pisa, Florence and Rome, where he discovered Michelangelo, of whom he said, "It is he who has freed me from academic sculpture."

1876   Returned to Belgium. *Joshua. The Vanquished*, the name of wich he later changed to *The Age of Bronze*.

1877   Controversy over *The Vanquished* in Brussels. Returned to Paris. Controversy over *The Age of Bronze. The Walking Man*.

1878   *The Man with the Broken Nose* rediscovered. Commissioned to make the great decorative scrolls on the Trocadéro for the World Fair.

1879   Carrier-Belleuse appointed director of the Sèvres porcelain works, hired him to design vases and cups (until 1882).

1880   Presentation of *St. John the Baptist Preaching* at the Salon. Purchase of *The Age of Bronze* by the French government. On August 16, Rodin received commission for *The Gates of Hell. The Thinker, and Adam or The First Man*.

1881   *The Three Shades, Eve, Ugolino, The Weeping Lion, Caryatid Carrying Her Stone*.

1882   *Pain, Crouching Woman*.

1882-83   Became acquainted with Léon Claudel's family. Met Gambetta, many politicians and Victor Hugo, of whom he sculpted a bust. Beginning of his passion for Camille Claudel, sister of the poet Paul Claudel and herself a sculptress.

1884-86   *The Burghers of Calais, Victor Hugo*.

1885   *Dawn*.

1886   *The Kiss*.

1888   Illustration of Baudelaire's "Les Fleurs du Mal" for the French publisher Gallimard. *The Walking Man* cast in bronze. Commissioned to make a monument to Victor Hugo.

1889   Monument to Claude Lorrain. Meeting with Medaro Rosso, followed by a quarrel, since both claimed to have been the first to use Impressionism in sculpture.

1890   Rodin told to revise his draft for the monument to Victor Hugo.

1891   Commissioned to make a monument to Balzac. Rodin was then 51, the age at wich the novelist died.

1893   Rodin due to complete his *Balzac*, which was by then in its naked, paunchy form. He refused to regard it as finished, and the "Balzac case" began.

1895   June 3. Erection and unveiling of *The Burghers of Calais* in their native town.

1897   Purchase of La Villa des Brillants at Meudon. Final version of *Balzac* (the Balzac Mountain). End of his liaison with Camille Claudel.

1898   Uproar over *Balzac* when it was rejected bu the Société des Gens de Lettres. Beginning of his monument to President Sarmiento in Buenos Aires.

1900   During the World Fair, Rodin showed two hundred works in a rotunda, among them *The Walking Man*.

1904   Rodin refunded the money paid by the French government for *The Gates of Hell*, the copyright of which he retained. Decoration of the entrance-hall of the villa La Sapinière at Evian.

1905   September. Rilke became his secretary, succeeding Charles Morice and Mario Meunier, one of the best translators of Plato. Of Rodin's assistant sculptors, three were to become famous — Popon, Bourdelle and Despiau.

1907   Went to live at the Hôtel Biron in Paris.

1908   Monument to Henri Becque.

1915   Second journey to Italy.

1917   February 14. Death of Marie-Rose Beuret, whom he had married some time previously. November 17, death of Rodin. December 22, Hôtel Biron made into a Rodin Museum.

NIGHT (1881-1882).   Porcelain vase, Manufacture de Sèvres h. 12⁷⁄₁₆″ (31.6 cm).   Musée Rodin, Paris

BIBLIOGRAPHY

ADAMS, Philip Rhys. *Auguste Rodin.* New York: Hyperion, 1945.

ALEXANDRE, Arsène. *Le Balzac de Rodin.* Paris: Floury, 1898.

AUBERT, Marcel *et al. Rodin, sculptures.* French and English. Paris: Tel, 1952.

AVELINE, Claude. *Rodin, l'homme et l'œuvre.* Paris: Les Ecrivains réunis, ca. 1927.

BARBIER, Nicole. *Marbres de Rodin. Collection du Musée.* Paris: Musée Rodin, 1987.

BEAUSIRE, Alain. *Les Expositions des sculptures de Rodin de son vivant.* Unpublished doctoral thesis, 1984.

BÉNÉDICTE, Léonce. *Rodin.* Tr. by Wilfrid Jackson. London: E. Benn, 1926.

BOEHMER, Günter. *Rodin.* Berlin: Wiese, 1938.

BORNIBUS, Jacques. *Auguste Rodin.* Paris: Galerie Claude Bernard, 1963.

BOURDELLE, Emile Antoine. *L'Art et Rodin.* Geneva, 1919.

BOURDELLE, Emile Antoine. *La Sculpture et Rodin.* Paris: Emile-Paul Frères, 1937.

BOUVY, Adrien. *Auguste Rodin.* Geneva, 1918.

BRECK, Joseph. *The Collection of Sculptures by Auguste Rodin.* New York: Metropolitan Museum of Art, 1913.

BÜNEMANN, Hermann. *Auguste Rodin, die Bürger von Calais.* Berlin: G. Maren 1946. Stuttgart: Reclam, 1957.

BUTLER, Ruth Mirolli. *The Early Works of Rodin and Its Background.* Revised edition of the author's doctoral thesis, New York University, 1966. Ann Arbor, Michigan: University Microfilms, 1966.

BUTLER, Ruth Mirolli *et al. Rodin in Perspective.* Englewood Cliffs, New Jersey: Prentice Hall, 1980.

CASSOU, Jean. *Rodin.* London, 1949.

CHAMPIGNEULLE, Bernard. *Rodin.* Tr. by Maxwell Brownjohn. London: Thames & Hudson, 1967. New York: Abrams, 1967. New York, Toronto: Oxford University Press, 1980.

CHARBONNEAUX, Jean. *Les Sculptures de Rodin.* Paris: Hazan, 1949.

CLADEL, Judith. *Le Sculpteur Auguste Rodin pris sur la vie.* Paris: La Plume, 1903.

CLADEL, Judith. *Rodin, l'œuvre et l'homme.* Tr. by S. K. Star. New York: The Century Co., 1917.

CLADEL, Judith. *Rodin, sa vie glorieuse, sa vie inconnue.* Tr. by James Withal. New York: Harcourt, Brace & Co.,1937 .

CLADEL, Judith. *Rodin.* Paris: Somogy, 1952.

COQUIOT, Gustave. *Le vrai Rodin.* Paris: Taillandier, 1913.

COQUIOT, Gustave. *Rodin à l'Hôtel Biron et à Meudon.* Paris: Ollendorf, 1917.

DAYOT, Armand. *Les Dessins de Rodin.* Paris, 1914.

DE CASO, Jacques. *Rodin's Thinker. Significant Aspects.* San Francisco, Californie: Fine Arts Museum, 1973.

DE CASO, Jacques and Patricia B. SANDERS. *Rodin's Sculpture: A critical study of the Spreckels Collection, California, Palace of the Legion of Honor.* San Francisco: Fine Arts Museum, 1977.

DESCHARNES, Robert et CHABRUN Jean-François. *Auguste Rodin.* Tr. by Edita Lausanne. New York: Viking, 1967. London: Macmillan, 1967.

DRIKS, Rudolf. *Auguste Rodin.* London: Siegle, Hill & Co., 1904.

DUHEM, Henri. *Auguste Rodin.* Paris, 1901.

DUJARDIN-BEAUMETZ, Etienne. *Entretiens avec Rodin.* Paris: Paul Dupont, 1913. Tr. and repr. in Elsen, Albert Edward, op. cit., 1965.

ELSEN, Albert Edward. *Rodin.* New York: Museum of Modern Art and Doubleday, 1963.

ELSEN, Albert Edward. *Auguste Rodin, Readings on his Life and Work.* Englewood Cliffs, New Jersey: Prentice Hall, 1965.

ELSEN, Albert Edward. *Rodin and Balzac. Rodin's Sculpture Studies for the Monument to Balzac from the Cantor-Fitzgerald Collection.* Beverly Hills, California: Cantor, Fitzgerald & Co., 1973.

ELSEN, Albert Edward. *In Rodin's Studio. A Photographic Record of Sculpture in the Making.* Oxford: Phaidon. Ithaca, New York: Cornell University Press, 1980.

ELSEN, Albert Edward. *The Gates of Hell by Auguste Rodin.* Stanford, California: Stanford University Press, 1985.

ELSEN, Albert Edward. *Rodin's Thinker and the Dilemmas of Modern Public Sculpture.* New Haven, Connecticut: Yale University Press, 1985.

ELSEN, Albert Edward *et al. The Drawings of Rodin.* New York: Praeger, 1972.

ELSEN, Albert Edward *et al. Rodin Rediscovered.* Washington, D.C.: National Gallery of Art, 1981.

EMDE, Ursula. *Rilke und Rodin.* Marburg, Lahn: Kunstgeschichtliche Seminare der Universität Marburg, 1948.

FEIST, Peter H., *et al. Auguste Rodin. Plastik, Zeichnungen, Graphik.* East-Berlin: Staatliche Museen, 1979.

FRISCH, Victor und Joseph T. SHIPLEY. *Auguste Rodin.* New York: Frederick A. Stockes Co., 1939.

GABERT, Roger. *Rodin inconnu.* Paris: L'Archipel, 1950.

GANTNER, Joseph. *Rodin und Michelangelo.* Vienna: A. Schroll, 1953.

GEFFROY, Gustave. *Auguste Rodin.* Paris: Dentu, 1892.

GEISSBUHLER, Elizabeth Chase. *Rodin, Later Drawings with Interpretations by Antoine Bourdelle.* Boston: Beacon Press, 1963.

GEYRAUD, Pierre. *Rodin devant la douleur et l'amour.* Paris, 1937.

GODSCHEIDER, Ludwig and STORY, Sommerville. *Rodin Sculpture.* New York: Dutton, 1979.

GOLDSCHEIDER, Cécile. *Aquarelles de Rodin.* Paris, 1948.

GOLDSCHEIDER, Cécile. *24 dessins de Rodin.* Paris, 1949.

GOLDSCHEIDER, Cécile. *Aquarelles et dessins de Rodin.* Paris, 1962.

GOLDSCHEIDER, Cécile. *Rodin, sa vie, son œuvre, son héritage.* Paris: Paris Productions, 1962-1963.

GOLDSCHEIDER, Cécile. *Rodin, Sculptures.* Paris: Hazan, 1964.

GOLDSCHEIDER, Cécile. *Danse, étude de Rodin.* Paris, 1967.

GRAPPE, Georges. *Le Musée Rodin.* Paris: Henri Laurens, 1934, 1944.

GRAUTOFF, Otto. *Auguste Rodin.* Bielefeld, Leipzig: Velhagen & Klasing, 1908.

GÜSE, Ernst-Gerhard, *et al. Auguste Rodin, Zeichnungen und Aquarelle.* Stuttgart: Hatje, 1984. Tr. by John Gabriel and Michael Taylor. *Auguste Rodin. Drawings and Watercolors.* New York: Rizzoli, 1985.

HALE, William Harlan. *The World of Rodin, 1840-1917.* New York. Time-Life Books, 1969.

HANOTELLE, Micheline. *Paris/Brüssel: Rodin et Meunier.* Paris: Le Temps, 1982.

HAVELAAR, Just. *Auguste Rodin.* Leiden, 1920. Utrecht, 1949.

HAWKINS, Jennifer. *Rodin Sculptures.* London: HMSO. Victoria and Albert Monographs, 30, 1975.

HINDENBURG, Helene von Nostitz. *Rodin in Gesprächen und Briefen von Helene von Nostitz.* Dresden: Wolfgang Jess, 1927. Dialogues with Rodin. New York, 1931.

JIANOU, Ionel und Cécile GOLDSCHEIDER. *Rodin.* Paris: Arted, 1968.

JOURDAIN, Francis. *Rodin.* Lausanne: Marguerat, 1949.

JUDRIN, Claudie. *Auguste Rodin, 100 Zeichnungen und Aquarelle.* Freiburg i. Br., Basel, Vienna: Herder, 1982.

JUDRIN, Claudie. *Inventaire des dessins: Musée Rodin.* Vol. I: *Les Centaures;* Vol. II: *Ugolin;* Vol. III: *Dante et Virgile aux Enfers.* Paris: Musée Rodin, 1981-1984.

LAMPERT, Catherine. *Rodin, Sculpiure and Drawings.* London: Arts Council of Great Britain, 1986.

LAURENT, Monique *et al. Le Musée Rodin.* Paris: Musée Rodin, 1977.

LAURENT, Monique et Claudie JUDRIN. *Rodin et les écrivains de son temps.* Paris: Musée Rodin, 1967.

LAURENT, Monique et Claudie JUDRIN. *Rodin et l'Extrême-Orient.* Paris: Musée Rodin, 1979.

LAURENT, Monique et Dominique VIEVILLE. *Rodin, le monument des Bourgeois de Calais.* Paris: Musée Rodin, 1978.

LAWTON, Frederick. *The Life and Work of Auguste Rodin.* London: Grant Richards, 1904, 1907; T. Fischer Unwin, 1906. New York: Scribner's & Sons, 1907.

LECOMTE, Georges Charles. *Chefs-d'œuvre de Rodin.* Paris: Publications techniques et artistiques, 1946.

LESLIE, Ann. *Rodin, The Immortal Peasant.* Englewood Cliffs, New Jersey: Prentice Hall, 1937. London: Herbert Joseph, 1939.

LUDOVICI, Anthony. *Personal Reminiscences of Auguste Rodin.* Philadelphia: Lippincott, 1926.

MAILLARD, Léon. *Auguste Rodin statuaire*. Paris: Floury, 1899.

MARTINIE, A. Henri. *Rodin*. Paris: Braun, 1947, 1952.

MARX, Roger. *Auguste Rodin*. Berlin, 1897.

MARX, Roger. *Les Pointes sèches de Rodin*. Paris, 1902.

MARX, Roger. *Auguste Rodin, céramiste*. Paris, 1907.

MAUCLAIR, Camille. *L'Œuvre de Rodin*. Paris: La Plume, 1900.

MAUCLAIR, Camille. *Auguste Rodin, l'homme et l'œuvre*. Tr. by Clementina Black. London: Duckworth, 1905..

McNAMARA, Mary Jo et Albert Edward ELSEN. *Rodin's Burghers of Calais*. New York: Cantor, Fitzgerald, 1977.

MILLER, Joan Vita et Gary MAROTTA. *Rodin: The B. Gerald Cantor Collection*. New York: Metropolitan Museum of Art, 1986.

MILLER, Joan Vita *et al. The Sculpture of Rodin. Reductions and Enlargements*. New York, 1983.

MIRBEAU, Octave, Stuart MERILL, et Camille MAUCLAIR. *Auguste Rodin et son œuvre*. Paris, 1900.

MORICE, Charles. *Rodin*. Paris: Floury, 1900.

MORTIER, Mme Alfred. *Rodin avant la femme, fragments inédits de Rodin, sa technique*. Paris, 1919.

PINET-CHEULA, Hélène. *Rodin sculpteur et les photographes de son temps*. Paris: P. Sers, 1985.

PLESSIER, Ghislaine. *Etude critique de la correspondance échangée entre Zuluoga et Rodin de 1903 à 1917*. Foreword by Bernard Dorival. Paris: Editions Hispaniques, 1983.

RAMBOSSON, Yvanhoé. *Le Modèle et le mouvement dans les œuvres de Rodin*. Paris: La Plume, 1900.

RILKE, Rainer Maria. *Auguste Rodin*. Berlin: Inselverlag, 1903. Leipzig, 1920. Tr. by Robert Firmage. Salt Lake City: Peregrino Smith, 1979.

RILKE, Rainer Maria. *Auguste Rodin dessinateur*. Vienne, n.d.

RILKE, Rainer Maria. *Lettres à Rodin*. Paris: Paul-Emile Frères, 1931.

RINALDINI, Julio. *Auguste Rodin*. Buenos Aires: Poseidon, 1942.

RIOTOR, Léon. *Rodin, statuaire, son œuvre et ses aventures. Rodin dessinateur, caractères et projets. Commentaires*. Paris, 1903.

RIOTOR, Léon. *Rodin*. Paris: Alcan, 1927.

ROH, Franz. *Rodin*. Bern: A. Scherz, 1949.

SCHILLING, Karl. *Auguste Rodins Vermächtnis in Gedanken und Gestaltung*. Hamburg: Hoffmann & Campe, 1939.

SCHMOLL VON EISENWERTH, J. Adolf. *Der Torso, Symbol und Form*. Bruno Grimm, 1954.

SCHMOLL VON EISENWERTH, J. Adolf. *Rodin-Studien: Persönlichkeit, Werke, Wirkung*. München: Prestel, 1983.

SELZ, Jean. "Rodin", in *Découverte de la sculpture moderne*. Lausanne: Guilde du Livre, 1963.

SIGOGNEAU, Albert. *A propos de Rodin*. Bordeaux: Imprimerie-Librairie de l'Université, 1932.

SPEAR, Athena Tacha. *Rodin Sculpture in the Cleveland Museum of Art*. Cleveland, Ohio: Museum of Art, 1967. Supplement, 1974.

SUTTON, Denys. *Triumphant Satyr. The World of Auguste Rodin*. London: Penguin, 1963. New York: Hawthorn Books, 1966.

SYMONS, Arthur. *From Toulouse-Lautrec to Rodin. With some personal impressions*. London: J. Lane, 1929.

TANCOCK, John. *The Sculpture of Auguste Rodin. The Collection of the Rodin Museum in Philadelphia*. Philadelphia: Museum of Art, 1976. Boston: D. Godine, 1976.

THORSON, Victoria. *The Late Drawings of Auguste Rodin*. Doctoral thesis. Ann Arbor: University of Michigan Press, 1973.

THORSON, Victoria. *Rodin's Graphics: A Catalogue Raisonné of Drypoints and Book Illustrations*. San Francisco: The Fine Arts Museum, 1975.

TIREL, Marcelle. *The last years of Rodin*. Tr. by René Francis. London: A. M. Philpot, 1922.

TUCKER, William. *The Language of Sculpture*. London: Thames & Hudson, 1974.

VARNEDOE, J. Kirk T. *Chronology and Authenticity in the Drawings by Auguste Rodin*. Unpublished doctoral thesis. Stanford University, California, 1972.

VEIDAUX, André. *Auguste Rodin statuaire*. Paris: Girard & Brière, 1900.

WALDMANN, Emil. *Auguste Rodin*. Vienna: A. Schroll, 1945.

WESTHEIM, Paul. *Künstlerbekenntnisse*. Berlin: Propyläen, n.d.

WRITINGS BY RODIN

"Gothic in the Churches and Cathedrals of France." Tr. by Frederick Lawton. In *The North American Review*, February 1905. The French original text is lost.

Rodin on Art. Interview by Paul Gsell. Tr. by Katherine Fedden. London, 1912. Boston: Small, Maynard & Co., 1912. New York: Philosophical Library, 1957.

Les Cathédrales de France. Foreword by Charles Morice. Paris: A. Colin, 1914.

Auguste Rodin. Briefe an zwei deutsche Frauen. Ed. by Helene von Nostitz. Berlin: Holle, 1936.

A la Venus de Milo. Foreword by A. Henri Martinie. Paris: La Jeune Parque, 1945.

Correspondance de Rodin. Ed. by Alain Beausire and Hélène Pinet. Vol. I: 1860-1899; Vol. II: 1900-1907. Paris: Musée Rodin, 1985-1986.

EXHIBITIONS

1963   *Auguste Rodin*. Catalogue by Albert Elsen. Museum of Modern Art, New York; California Palace of the Legion of Honor, San Francisco.

1963-1964   *Auguste Rodin 1840-1917. An Exhibition of Sculptures and Drawings*. Introduction by Leo Steinberg, catalogue by Cécile Goldscheider. Slatkin Galleries, New York; Museum of Fine Arts, Montreal; The Art Gallery of Toronto; Museum of Art, Cleveland; Museum of Art, Baltimore.

1964   *Line and Wash Drawings by Auguste Rodin. Collection of Dr. and Mrs. Lincoln M. Polan*. Museum of Fine Art, Houston.

1965   *Auguste Rodin*. Ateneumin Taidemuseo, Helsinki; Museum of Fine Arts, Turku; Museum of Fine Arts, Tampere.

1966   *Rodin*. National Museum, Stockolm.
Rodin. Arts Council of Great Britain, London.
Rodin. Roland, Browse and Delbanco Galleries, London.
Rodin. Catalogue by Cécile Goldscheider. National Museum of Western Art, Tokyo; Museum of the City of Kyoto; Cultural Center, Fukuoka.

1966-1967   *Rodin and His Contemporaries*. National Gallery of South Australia, Adelaide; Queen Victoria Museum and Art Gallery, Lanceston.

1967   *Auguste Rodin*. Académie de France, Villa Medici, Rome.
Rodin. Foreword by Cécile Goldscheider. Museum of Arts, Tel Aviv.
Rodin et les écrivains de son temps. Catalogue by Monique Laurent and Claudie Judrin. Musée Rodin, Paris.

1967-1968   *Homage to Rodin. Collection of B. Gerald Cantor*. Intoduction and catalogue by Cécile Goldscheider. Los Angeles County Museum of Art.

1968   *Rodin collectionneur*. Catalogue by Cécile Goldscheider. Musée Rodin, Paris.

1969   *Rodin Bronzes from the Collection of B. Gerald Cantor*. American Federation of Arts.
The Partial Figure in Modern Sculpture from Rodin to 1969. Catalogue by Albert Elsen. Museum of Art, Baltimore.

1970   *Rodin and His Contemporaries*. Museum of Fine Arts, Montreal.
Rodin. Sculptures and Drawings. Catalogue by Alan Bowness and Andrew Dempsey. Hayward Gallery, London.

1971 *Arp and Rodin*. Text by Albert Elsen. Feingarten Galleries, Los Angeles.
Rodin. Esculturas, acuarelas y dibujos. Museo de Bellas Artes, Caracas.
Auguste Rodin from the B. Gerald Cantor Collection and the B. Gerald Cantor Foundation. William Rockhill Nelson Gallery and Mary Atkins Museum of Fine Arts, Kansas City, Missouri.

1971-1972 *Rodin Drawings, True and False*. Catalogue by Albert Elsen and Kirk Varnedoe. National Gallery of Art, Washington, D.C.

1972 *Rodin*. Roland, Browse and Delbanco Galleries, London.

1973 *Rodin's Thinker*. Catalogue by Jacques De Caso. California Palace of the Legion of Honor, San Francisco.
Rodin and Balzac. Rodin's Sculptural Studies for the Monument to Balzac. Catalogue by Albert Elsen, Stephen C. McGough, and Steven H. Wander. Cantor, Fitzgerald & Co., Beverly Hills, California.

1975 *Rodin Graphics*. A catalogue raisonné of drypoints and book illustrations by Victoria Thorson. California Palace of the Legion of Honor, San Francisco.
Rodin Sculptures. Victoria and Albert, London.

1976 *Rodin. The Maryhill Collection: Bronzes, Plasters, Watercolors*. Paul Getty Museum, Malibu, California.
Rodin. Catalogue by Monique Laurent and Claudie Judrin. Seibu Galleries, Tokyo.
Rodin. Catalogue used for the exhibition: Albert Elsen, *Rodin and Balzac, Rodin's Sculpture Studies fron the Monument to Balzac from the Cantor-Fitzgerald Collection*. New York, 1974. Museum of Modern Art, New York.
Rodin et les écrivains de son temps. Catalogue par Monique Laurent et Claudie Judrin. Musée Rodin, Paris.

1977 *Rodin's Burghers of Calais*. Catalogue essays by Mario Jo McNamara and Albert Elsen. Beverly Hills, California.

1978 *Rodin and His Contemporaries. Sculptures from the Burrel Collection*. Art Gallery, Glasgow.
Auguste Rodin. Le Monument des Bourgeois de Calais dans les collections du Musée Rodin et du Musée des Beaux-Arts de Calais. Catalogue by Claudie Judrin, Monique Laurent and Dominique Vieville. Musée des Beaux-Arts, Calais.

1979 *Rodin et l'Extrême-Orient*. Catalogue by Claudie Judrin and Monique Laurent. Musée Rodin, Paris.

Auguste Rodin. Plastik, Zeichnungen, Graphik. Catalogue edited by Peter H. Feist. Staatliche Museen, East-Berlin.

1980 *The Romantics to Rodin*. Catalogue edited by Peter Fusco and H.W. Janson. Los Angeles County Museum of Art.
Rodin. Skulpturen, Zeichnungen, eine Ausstellung des Musée Rodins, Paris, und des Collectors Club, Wien. Catalogue by Gerhard Habarta. Orangerie, Vienna.
Auguste Rodin. Institute of Arts, Flint, Michigan.

1981 *Les Centaures*. Drawings compiled by Claudie Judrin. Musée Rodin, Paris.

1981-1982 *Rodin Rediscovered*. Catalogue edited by Albert Elsen. National Gallery of Art, Washington, D.C.

1982 *Rodin Bronzes*. Bruton Galleries, Brussels, London. Galerie Valentien, Stuttgart.

1982-1983 *Ugolin*. Drawings compiled by Claudie Judrin. Musée Rodin, Paris.

1983 *Dante et Virgile aux Enfers*. Drawings compiled by Claudie Judrin. Musée Rodin, Paris.
Rodin and the French Genius: 100 Years of Figurative Sculpture. Bruton Galleries, London.
Rodin and His Contemporaries. Barbican Center for Arts and Conferences, Barbican Art Gallery, London.

1984 *Rodin*. Fondation Pierre Giannada, Martigny, Switzerland.
Controversial Public Art from Rodin to di Suvero. Introduction by Gerald Nordland. Milwaukee Art Museum, Wisconsin.
Rodin, les mains, les chirurgiens. Catalogue by Monique Laurent, Michel Merle, and Danièle Gutmann. Musée Rodin, Paris.
Camille Claudel. Catalogue by Monique Laurent and Michel Merle. Musée Rodin, Paris.

1984-1985 *Auguste Rodin. Zeichnungen und Aquarelle*. Catalogue by E.G. Güse *et al.* Westfälisches Landesmuseum für Kunst und Kulturgeschichte, Münster, Federal Republic of Germany.

1985 Camille Claudel - Auguste Rodin. Künstlerpaare - Künstlerfreunde. Texts by Judith Cladel *et al.* Kunstmuseum, Bern.

1986 *Rodin: The B. Gerald Cantor Collection*. Catalogue by Joan Vita Miller and Gary Marotta. Metropolitan Museum of Art, New York.

1986-1987 *Rodin. Sculpture and Drawings*. Catalogue by Catherine Lampert. Hayward Gallery, London.

We wish to thank the owners of the works reproduced in this book.

DENMARK: Ny Carlsberg Glyptotek, Copenhagen

FRANCE: Musée Rodin, Meudon
                 Musée Bourdelle, Paris
                 Musée d'Orsay, Paris
                 Petit-Palais, Paris
                 Musée Rodin, Paris

UNITED STATES: Museum of Fine Arts, Boston
                 The Art Institute, Chicago
                 The Metropolitan Museum of Art, New York
                 Rodin Museum, Philadelphia
                 Toledo Museum of Art, Ohio

SUISSE: The Thyssen-Bornemisza Collection, Lugano-Castagnola, Switzerland

The photographs of the illustrations on the following pages:
15, 16, 22, 23, 24, 30, 32, 51, 57, 75 and 87 were taken by Studio Lourmel, Paris.

ILLUSTRATIONS